The Noonday Devil

The Noonday Devil

Alan Judd

Hutchinson
London Melbourne Auckland Johannesburg

This edition first published in 1987 by Hutchinson, an imprint
of Century Hutchinson Ltd, Brookmount House, 62–65
Chandos Place, London WC2N 4NW
Century Hutchinson Australia Pty Ltd
PO Box 496, 16–22 Church Street, Hawthorn, Victoria 3122,
Australia
Century Hutchinson New Zealand Limited
PO Box 40–086, Glenfield, Auckland 10, New Zealand
Century Hutchinson South Africa (Pty) Ltd
PO Box 337, Berglvei, 2012 South Africa
Printed and bound in Great Britain by
Anchor Brendon Ltd, Tiptree, Essex

British Library Cataloguing in Publication Data
Judd, Alan
  The noonday devil.
  I. Title
  823'.914[F]   PR6060.U32

ISBN 0–09–168180–2

'Now comth wanhope, that is despair of the mercy of God' Geoffrey Chaucer, *The Parson's Tale*

'Shame on the soul, to falter on the road of life, while the body still perserveres' Marcus Aurelius, *Meditations*

My thanks to Hugh Baker, Richard Cohen, Richard
Holmes and Peter Scrafton

Chapter One

It was very hot during that final term and the mist on May morning was low, white and heavy. Roofs and towers stretched above it to the sun.

In a basement lumber room, lit by a yellow bulb, Robert Stephens sat working at an old table that wobbled with each movement of his arm. There was a heap of broken and discarded college furniture in one half of the room and in another corner a pile of stiff, cracked grey canvas. Heating pipes ran the length of the ceiling. The empty half of the room had been used for a play rehearsal which had begun at eight o'clock the previous evening and had not ended until gone three. Everyone, including Robert, had been exhausted, but while the others had gone gratefully to bed he had remained, tired beyond sleep and anyway too anxious. He covered his tattered script with notes, crossings out, arrows and directions.

The play was not going well. Time and again he saw where it was wrong but nothing he did made it come right. He knew, of course, that plays went through troughs in rehearsal and that directors went through times of despair. He told himself he had only to keep going, and did so, but still it would not come right.

Daylight paled the dirty window panes just above ground level, showing the tiredness in his face. It was a strong face, freckled, gashed by a big mouth and topped by thick brown hair. He was powerfully built, but his hands were small and delicately formed and his eyes grey and thoughtful. In repose he had a brooding quality, an idle power, careless and decisive. His gaze now was as

1

blank as the mist he stared at. He was a man withdrawn beyond reach, sunk in upon himself. Eventually he got up and slowly gathered his papers. His chair fell over behind him.

Robert had rooms in the roof of the Old Building. They were at the top of a cramped staircase and were poky and awkward, hot in summer, cold in winter. He managed to make them both sparse and untidy. Most of his clothes were in an open trunk on the floor, his books piled on and beneath his table. There were no paintings or posters nor any sign of anything personal. The impression was of cheerless and temporary occupancy, like a barracks in the process of abandonment.

It was not yet six. From his window he could look down on the yellow brickwork of the New Building. The sun was already pressing against the closed blinds of the box-like rooms on the upper storey. Below and beyond, the city was as silent as if the mist was a flood.

He moved about the room in restless indecision, several times returning to the window. He switched on a battered portable radio which, after initial crackling, promised yet another account of the worsening international situation. In grave tones betrayed by a relish for sensation the announcer held out the prospect of Russian and American fighters clashing over Saudi Arabia. Robert switched it off and ran downstairs, not bothering to close his door.

He walked quickly through the deserted streets. The mist was like dense white smoke but cold and damp on the skin. The May morning ceremony took place at six on Magdalen Bridge. People gathered to hear the college choir sing a hymn from the top of the tower. The rest of the day was an unofficial holiday. There was no traffic at all that morning, though as Robert approached the High he saw other hurrying, solitary walkers, then a few pairs, then a group. All moved quickly and quietly, without speaking.

By the time he reached the bridge two or three thousand people were packed together there, either on the bridge

2

itself or on the road leading to it. They stood in silence, looking up, the only sounds the footsteps of those still joining. Below them the Cherwell flowed out of and into its own river mist; above, the top of Magdalen Tower was just becoming visible. There were no cars, hardly any movement, only a hushed expectant stillness. The mist lifted moment by moment. Robert looked over the heads of those around him. He was pressed against the wall by a girl with red hair. Through her thin cotton dress he could feel the warmth of her body. When she shifted slightly she glanced, half smiled, then resumed her gaze upwards.

The bells struck the hour and the mist abruptly cleared from the top of the tower, as if dispersed by the sound. Throughout the city other bells joined in. One, far away, insisted on another time altogether. As the last chime faded the choir on the top of the tower, invisible and at first barely audible, began singing the May morning hymn. Packed elbow to elbow, thigh to thigh, no one moved. The sun touched the tower and the voices of the unseen choir came thinly, hauntingly down.

As soon as the hymn had finished the crowd began to break up. Some arranged to have breakfast or go punting, a few went off to work. Robert walked slowly between the various groups, nodding to people he knew but talking to no one until he came upon Tim Albright. Tim was tall and strikingly pale with dark hair and sharp, humorous features. He wheeled an expensive black Raleigh, newly made in an old fashioned style.

Tim smiled. 'Breakfast?'

'Bed.'

'You looking for someone in particular?'

'No.'

Tim leaned with graceful indolence against his bike. 'I came round to your room but you'd already gone — or else you hadn't yet got back.'

'Rehearsing.'

'You're off your head.'

3

Robert nodded. Though they lived on adjacent staircases and had known each other for nearly three years,
they had become friends only at the start of their final
year. Superficially they had little in common. Tim read
philosophy, had been to public school, had a twice-
divorced mother and a stepfather who was a well-known
captain of industry. Wealthy, likeable and clever, he
seemed entirely lacking in ambition and had achieved
everything, including his scholarship, without effort.
Now, with the approach of Schools — the name given
both to final examinations and the buildings they were
held in — he seemed even less concerned with work than
before. Sometimes at night when the streets were quiet
he would freewheel on his Raleigh, seeing how far he
could go before falling off. He claimed to be trying to put
into practice a mathematical relation between gradient,
mass and velocity.

Robert read theology and came from Cumbria where
his father was a postman. Though he had never spoken
much about it, people assumed he was going into the
Church. He had worked hard at school and during his
first two years at Oxford, achieving an exhibition and a
regular place in the college first teams for rugby and
cricket. He had been expected to get a rugby Blue in his
third year but he had abruptly given up the game at the
start of the season. He displayed the same energy and
drive as before but his direction was no longer clear. He
had become restless, substituted drama for sport, and did
little work.

His manner that morning was remote and unrespon-
sive, due partly to tiredness. Tim almost never took
offence.

'Anne Barry was here,' he said.

'Was she?'

'On the bridge about a minute ago. Heading towards
Longwall Street, I imagine. No husband in sight.' He
watched Robert's studied lack of reaction. 'You're more
in luck this morning than I am. I'd arranged to meet

4

Suzanne. Thought she probably wouldn't turn up, but to bolster my confidence I bet a bottle of malt on it with Chetwynd. He's here somewhere.'

'You're sure she isn't?'

'Pretty sure. Unless Chetwynd's kidnapped her. He's crazy enough.'

'I suppose it's too early to go to her room.'

'I was thinking I might, if I could find a way in. Shouldn't be too difficult. Fancy it? Or are you going to try to breakfast with Mrs Barry?'

Robert smiled at the transparency of his own motive.

'Haven't seen her for a couple of weeks.'

'When's she going to make Dr Barry a father?'

'Very soon. A month, maybe. Maybe less.'

'He's already a father about nine times, isn't he, by his first wife?'

'Something like that.'

Robert turned to go but lingered awkwardly, wanting to show gratitude by making a parting remark but momentarily unable to think of one. 'Sooner him than me,' he said lamely. 'Good luck in your search.'

'Sooner anyone. Drop in later.'

Robert blamed himself for the break-up of his affair with Anne Barry. It had lasted for most of his second year. She, a year older than him, had stayed on to do research. He blamed himself for the break because it was easier than acknowledging the whole truth. He would say that he had been too selfish and demanding, driving her from him. This was less painful than admitting that he had felt she was beginning to withdraw anyway. At a certain point in their intimacy he had sensed a distance between them which had widened. For some reason that she could not or would not explain, she had stepped carefully backwards.

Within a week of their last night together she had taken up with Dr Barry, the college's philosophy tutor and her research supervisor. He was nearly twenty years older than her, had already left his first wife and was popularly

5

supposed to be having an affair with the Bursar's pretty secretary. This supposition, based on the frequency of their lunches together out of college and on his known flirtatiousness, had been confounded by his sudden marriage to Anne and by her evident pregnancy. More recently the lunches, which had never entirely ceased, had resumed their previous frequency.

Robert found Anne that morning among the people loitering by Magdalen wall. She was a tall, handsome woman with strong regular features and dark brown hair that spread over her bare shoulders. Her arms and legs were brown with the sun and she wore a flowery cream maternity dress. Her manner in pregnancy had become calm and self-absorbed. When she saw him walk towards her she at first turned away, then looked back with a more prepared expression and a smile.

'I thought you might be here,' she said.

'I thought you might.' There was a momentary awkwardness when they might have touched. 'Pretty good, wasn't it?'

'It was beautiful. I heard more this year than last.'

'There was that wind last year.'

'Yes.'

'You're looking well.'

'Thank you.'

'It suits you.'

She looked down at herself. 'It will suit me better when it's over.'

He had always felt uneasy in her presence, and reacted now with exaggerated carelessness. 'Why don't we have breakfast?'

'I'm supposed to be going to my cousin's. You know, Michael Mann.'

'Okay.'

'But it's a party. There'll be a lot of people, you know what he's like. Why don't you come?'

'Okay.'

They walked slowly through Magdalen cloisters and

quad. Half the college seemed to be up and out for break-fast. There was an air of bustling goodwill.

'You look tired,' she said.

'I've been up all night rehearsing.'

'You're mad to do a play in Schools term.'

'It passes the time.'

'I don't believe that's why you're doing it.' She looked thoughtfully at him. 'Are you doing any work at all?'

'Not much. Nor's Tim,' he added, as if in exoneration. 'Neither of us has any idea what to do when we leave.' He kicked a stone along the cloisters. 'Not that it matters much to him, with his money.'

'Well, you'll get your degree. Everyone does. Just not as good as you could get, that's all.'

'How's David?'

'Very well.' She smiled quickly. 'I left him in bed. I don't think he's had to get up early since he was at school. He was quite incredulous when I said I was coming here.'

'He didn't mind — doesn't mind you doing things?'

'Not at all. Far from it.'

The party was in first floor rooms. They could hear it before entering the building. 'This will probably be awful,' she said. 'All Michael's acting friends. We don't have to stay long.'

'You say you're tired and I'll say I have to walk you home.'

'That'll give them something to gossip about.' Seeing him smile, she laid her hand on his arm. 'It's nice that we can talk like this now, isn't it?'

About twenty people were sitting on the floor, balancing on the arms and backs of chairs, standing outside on the narrow balcony. The host, Michael Mann, was the most successful drama director in Oxford. Fat and voluble, he had thick black hair, wore thick gold rings and talked about drama with such commanding fluency that in his presence it was hard to believe anything else mattered. He had had two productions at the Playhouse, the premier theatre in Oxford, and was currently rehearsing *A Midsummer Night's Dream* for Worcester College gardens. Endowed with surpassing energy, he slept little, read everything, knew everyone, and apparently had no private life at all. His life was like his drama, public property, a matter for debate, open to revision, in need of presentation. Hardly a week passed without his giving a party of some kind. He greeted Anne with open arms but embraced her gently.

'I thought you were never coming, that perhaps you were deterred by disapproval, donnish and uxorious.'

'At this time of day there's no question of approval or disapproval, donnish or otherwise. He's blissfully indifferent to whatever I get up to.'

He nodded at Robert with off-handed affability. 'So you brought an understudy?'

Robert assumed equal affability. 'I created the part in rep.' It was always important to repay Michael early on and in kind, after which he would usually take no further interest. It was not that he and Robert were serious rivals in drama or anything else — Robert's theatrical ventures had been too infrequent and maverick for that — but rather that Michael established relations with people in terms of degrees of ascendancy. He would assume as much as he was permitted; it was for them to establish the limits. Few did so.

Michael waved his arms again. 'Champagne, orange, coffee, croissants. Help yourselves.'

Anne knew some of the others; Robert was on nodding terms with most but was not anxious to get better acquainted. He felt he knew enough people. Anne accepted orange juice and a seat from a cheerful man who helped himself and everyone else to more champagne.

'I'm going to drink this stuff every day until war breaks out,' the man said. 'At least I'll enjoy myself first and I'd rather die gloating about that than feeling bitter and twisted because I hadn't.'

'You might feel worse for knowing what you're

missing,' said a pretty girl in white boots, jeans, jersey and hat.

Michael joined them. 'The answer, surely, is to make the most of the actual experience of being fried. I mean, if I had warning of imminent nuclear attack I'd rush into the garden with my deckchair, put on Beethoven's Ninth and sit back and watch for the big flash. Uplifting in every way.'

Most people laughed. Robert smiled when he saw that Anne had.

'In fact, I'm more worried about rain during *The Dream* week than nuclear war,' continued Michael. 'I mean, it's one thing for everyone to be annihilated, quite another if it's only the audience.'

There was more laughter, then talk about what else would be worth doing before war broke out, though carried on in a way that suggested no one believed it would. The cheerful man told the girl in white that he would hope to spend more time in bed.

Robert and Anne left after about half an hour amid jokes about Anne having to wake her husband. Michael asked Robert how *The Changeling* was going and Robert asked after *The Dream*. They had a brief and businesslike exchange, Michael's way of showing goodwill.

'Don't forget the madhouse scenes,' he said. 'Very tempting to leave them until it's too late. I nearly did that for a school production. Great theatrical possibilities. Anne, we must have tea.'

She said tea would be lovely at any time but escaped without being specific.

The relief on leaving was as much physical as mental. The sun was already warm and the streets were busier. Her brown eyes rested on his for a moment.

'You didn't have to leave with me,' she said. 'All those lovely girls. You should have stayed.'

'I'd sooner have breakfast than be it.'

'David would have been in his element. It's about the

only thing he'd get up early for. Doesn't know what he missed.'

Anne and David lived in Norham Gardens, so she and Robert headed up past Keble. There was an old Daimler Majestic parked in a side road but she wanted to go through the parks, so he had to confine himself to a lingering look. The parks were empty save for a solitary jogger. The grass was wet and the dew glistened on the Japanese miniature trees.

'Do you still go for your runs?' she asked.

'Yes, every day now.'

'That's a bit much, isn't it? Why so often?'

'If I didn't overdo it I wouldn't do it at all.'

'I think that's rather suspicious. It's also rather typical.'

They walked slowly, her sandals making a soft sound in the grass.

'Still the same date?' he asked.

'Of course it's the same. It's an estimate. It may be right or wrong but it doesn't change.'

'I keep thinking of it as the projected arrival date for a round the world yacht race. You know, something that changes with the conditions.'

'Just as well it doesn't.' The jogger padded past them. 'Do you go much faster than that?'

'Depends how much I want to hurt myself.'

She laughed. 'Oh, dear.'

Within sight of the Cherwell they turned into a passage that gave on to the front of Lady Margaret Hall. A bald, irritible-looking man in a car asked them the way to the Cherwell Boat House. Anne directed him, leaning forward with one hand on the car and the other on her stomach. She was elegant and decisive, which made Robert feel superfluous.

'I had breakfast there with Tim on Sunday,' he said afterwards. 'He's been there every Sunday this term. Always takes someone. It starts at midday so you punt for an hour or two first and then come in and have fried eggs with black sausages and brandy and coffee and the

10

papers. Nice way to start the day. In fact, it fills it. You're no good for anything else.' He glanced quickly at her, trying to remember whether he had talked in the same terms the previous year or had perhaps even been there with her. 'Why don't you come next Sunday? If you're not doing anything.'

She did not look up. 'You're very eclectic, you and Tim. It's strange because you don't have much else in common. You both collect sensations. Yet you always seem remote and detached, separate from them, even when you say you enjoy them.'

He raised his eyes to the blue above the rooftops. 'I need notice of remarks like that.'

'The trouble is, it encourages other people to take the same attitude towards you.' She took his arm. 'Don't worry, only teasing. I wouldn't say it if I — if I didn't know you well.'

It was a quiet street of substantial Edwardian houses and overgrown gardens. Hers, partly hidden by a tree, had a broken gate and a crumbling wall. In the garden were bikes belonging to the student lodgers they took in to help Dr Barry with his maintenance payments.

'Come in and have some proper breakfast,' she said. 'No brandy, though.'

David Barry was sitting in the large untidy kitchen eating toast and reading the *Guardian*. He was a lively, iconoclastic Welshman with a restless energy, nervous and intellectual. His eyes were never still and he was renowned for his quick tongue, though his wit was perhaps due not so much to his being more perceptive than other people as less kind. He taught philosophy, in which Robert was to sit one paper. He greeted them both now with abrupt and impersonal cheerfulness.

'It won't bite, Robert, it's only Nescafé. Sit down.'

It was not the first time Robert had been with the two of them together. He did not fear or dislike it but found, slightly to his irritation, that he still talked with unusual rapidity as if to avoid gaps. He wondered if they did the

11

same. They discussed the May morning ceremony and the party. Dr Barry agreed that he would have liked the girls and smiled mischievously. Robert talked about his play, partly because it was something he could talk about and partly to avoid discussing work, until it struck him that it might well prompt the question. After that they talked about the international situation. A plump girl wearing a Yale T-shirt walked in, said 'Hi' three times, took a carton of milk from the fridge and walked out.

'That's Yale Gail,' said Dr Barry. 'Doing Early Middle Ages, like her waistline.' Anne sighed and said she wished he wouldn't. He went on talking and reading the paper simultaneously, peppering his conversation with comments about the Government. His and Anne's remarks to each other were few and off-hand, almost curt, a habit that Robert had at first thought was marriage shorthand for an understanding already reached. Anne's manner was colder and sharper than usual.

When she presented her cheek for Robert's goodbye kiss she seemed perfunctory and distracted. He did not respond but stepped back, forcing her to look at him.

'Thank you,' he said.

'Lovely to see you.'

'Are you all right?'

She kissed him directly on the lips. 'Sweet of you to ask.'

On leaving Robert, Tim had paused on Magdalen Bridge to look at the water. He never crossed a bridge without doing so, and he stared for some minutes at the slow eddies before pushing his bike towards St Hilda's College. He chained the bike to a railing some distance from the porter's lodge. The iron gates were locked but there was a smaller side gate that was not. No porter was evident. Once through the gate he quickly crossed the wet lawn towards one of the newer residential buildings. The door was locked. After looking around for a few seconds, he climbed the adjacent garden wall and pulled himself up to an open first-floor window that gave on to the stairs.

Inside he moved swiftly up two more flights and into one of the carpeted corridors where he paused and listened, very slightly out of breath. There was no sound of anyone stirring nor of anyone in the loo. He walked to the door at the end, cautiously turned the handle and stepped inside. There was a close, cloying feminine smell and he could hear breathing. His heart thumped against his ribs but his mind was filled with a fatalistic calm.

Her bed was round the corner. He stepped softly forward and paused. Suzanne lay curled up on her side, the blankets thrown off and only a sheet covering her. Her hips bulged surprisingly and her black hair was spread across the pillow. Her breathing was regular, her pale face half-hidden by her forearm. He sat carefully on the edge of the bed, whispered her name, waited, then spoke it. He put his hand on her shoulder, feeling the warmth of her skin and the slight rise and fall of her body. Sparrows squabbled on the windowsill and in the street someone started a car. After a while he withdrew his hand and very delicately pulled up the sheet so that it covered her shoulder. On the way out he noticed two pairs of her tights hanging to dry over the sink. He stopped and tied all four legs together, taking some minutes to form two linked bows, before creeping back down the corridor.

In the late afternoon the sun filled Robert's room with a warm glow before sinking behind the New Building. The skyline beyond was formed by Wytham Wood, and when the sun sank beneath it the sky became a vivid red with ragged shreds of clouds scattered as if by a bomb burst.

Robert stood in the exact centre of his room, staring through the window at the denizens of the New Building, whom he could study like zoo animals. He pressed with both hands on the pile of unread books on the table before him until roused by the college clock striking the quarter.

He went into his bedroom, changed hurriedly into running kit, loped across the quad, dodged the people milling about the porter's lodge proffering leaflets and exaltations about Saudi Arabia and headed up towards the parks.

He always ran alone and for anything between twenty minutes and an hour. It was partly because he had acquired the habit of fitness, partly because it brought mental relief. It was not possible to think when out of breath.

Once through the parks he crossed the Cherwell on an arched bridge and ran along the bank, then cut away down a cattle track by a hedge. The ground was hard and rugged and the cropped grass patchy and brown. The willow-lined ditches were dry.

The real satisfaction, the punishment, came when he was over the bridge and on the way back. He sprinted the last quarter-mile or so. To keep going he concentrated on each straining muscle in turn, identifying and separating the pain, making it an object of study. Over the last hundred yards it was the tightness in his chest and the leaden reluctance of his thighs that were most insistent. He pushed and pushed again, knowing his body would go faster if only he made it.

When at last he tottered through the park gates relief did not come instantly. But the knowledge that it would within seconds was the best part, better than the relief itself because that was valued less the more it was felt. He knew the whole business took a measure of self-hatred; a thought he did not find displeasing.

Chapter Two

In the hall that night Robert was not in the speaking mood. He sat with his shoulders hunched and his elbows on the table, turning his dessert spoon over and over. His gown was filthy, a result not only of neglect but also of the custom of wearing gowns as protection against the soup and gravy liberally spilled by the waiters and waitresses. The college had decided by referendum the year before that gowns should remain compulsory at dinner. In any case, a dirty gown was a sign of seniority.

Dinner was both formal and hurried. The undergraduates sat at long benches, elbow to elbow, in a discomfort that did not encourage lingering. Table lamps left the beamed roof and portraits of presidents and benefactors in cavernous gloom. There was a minstrels' gallery, used now for storing chairs and occasionally for a college drama production.

Robert had kept a place beside him. Tim slipped into it with the briefest glance of acknowledgement just before Mr Farrow, the butler, announced the entrance of High Table. The two hundred or so gowned figures then stood at their benches, looking from behind like beetles balanced on their tails, while the dons walked the length of the hall, shoes creaking, gowns rustling. When they were assembled at high table the President nodded to a classics scholar who stood at the head of the nearest of the low tables. The scholar read the grace in Latin, everyone sat and the hubbub resumed.

It was green pea soup again. Robert said nothing as the bowl was almost thrown in front of him, heaving like

15

some primeval matter. As always, he seemed indifferent to food, eating anything and never commenting, perhaps never noticing. He was sometimes abstracted, sometimes aggressively energetic, remote and intense by turn.

Tim also contemplated his soup in silence. Alone among undergraduates he had his gown cleaned regularly and wore a tie for dinner. Despite his attempts to make meals bearable, though, college food remained the greatest test of his willingness to accept college life. The unremitting stodginess, ubiquitous sprouts, unconquerable meat, the smell of centuries of communal cooking seeping from the stones and woodwork and the sheer noise of students feeding had more than once driven him to seek lodgings outside; but always he came back. He seemed to like to feel a part of it all, though he took very little part in it, and in any case could well afford to eat out whenever he liked.

The soup bowls were cleared away and the dinner plates banged down. Robert started fiddling with his spoon again. Tim stared at High Table, still silent but suddenly attentive.

'See the lady?' he asked eventually.

Robert looked in vain. It was a night when undergraduates were not allowed guests.

'High Table, next to the Chaplain,' added Tim.

The line of donnish faces, variously battered, was softened in the centre by a very pretty young woman with shining black hair tied in a bun. She wore subfusc, which was black skirt and gown, white blouse and black bow tie. On her left was the college President, on her right the Chaplain, who was almost as pretty in a different way. It took Robert a moment or two to recognize Suzanne.

'Did you know she was coming?' he asked.

'No.'

'But what's she doing on High Table? Did the Chaplain invite her?'

'Looks like it.'

'Well, that should be reassuring.'

16

'She goes for the religious. There's that monk at Christ Church.'

'Did you see her this morning?'

'That was all. I didn't wake her.' Tim's manner was ironic, self-deprecating. He appeared deliberately to undercut whatever seriousness he might feel about anything.

'Very romantic of you,' said Robert after a while.

'That's what I thought. I'd like her to know about it but if I had to tell her it would spoil it. I left a small sign of my presence, though.'

A hunk of bread landed on the table and another hit the wall behind, followed by a cheer from one of the tables by the door. It was becoming a rowdy night. Someone was sconced during the main course. The banging of spoons on tables while the man who was challenged stood on his bench and downed his beer put an end to all conversation. Years of the custom had flattened the bottom of college spoons; another cause of spillage.

'They hardly ever do it properly,' said a bespectacled mathematician called Marlowe. 'You're supposed to have to apply to High Table in a classical tongue for permission to sconce and they have to reply in a classical tongue. If your challenger is junior to you in college or is sitting farther than you from High Table you may apply to be released from the sconce. In a classical tongue, of course. People never seem to bother.'

'Any classical tongue?' asked a small dark man called Orpwood. 'Classical Chinese?'

'If you like; at High Table they may respond in whichever they choose. Tonight it will doubtless be Latin since the President will take it upon himself and his Greek is notorious.'

Orpwood nodded. He lived on Robert's staircase, had bulging dark eyes, was balding prematurely and was often mimicked because of his high eager voice. He belonged to a Marxist group opposed to Western inter-

17

vention in the Middle Eastern crisis. During his first two years he had been much mocked but by the third his humourless persistence and refusal to be daunted had wearied his detractors. Few people were seriously interested in politics, anyway, and there were others besides Orpwood to laugh at or argue about. His doggedness won acceptance, even respect. While the spoon-banging increased in rhythm and volume he studied a sheet of paper, surreptitiously at first. When the sconcing was finished and the cheers had died down he addressed those near him.

'Would you be willing to sign this manifesto for peace? It's part of the international student campaign to put pressure on capitalist governments to keep out of the Middle East. The more signatures we can get the more chance of persuading our own government not to drag us into nuclear war.'

'What about the Russians?' asked Marlowe. 'Are you petitioning them not to interfere in the Middle East?'

'It's an international campaign, as I said, and the Soviet student organization is bringing pressure to bear on the Soviet government.' The attempt to be both discreet and urgent made Orpwood's voice squeak.

'I don't believe that.'

'That's because you don't want to.' Orpwood waved his petition across the table. 'Look, what I'm talking about is the choice between staying alive and nuclear annihilation. What's the point of everyone being killed? What's worth dying for? Not a few barrels of oil — no one believes that. Anyway, the Third World needs the oil more than we do. We're robbing them of their resources.'

Marlowe shook his head. 'What rubbish. We're not robbing anyone of anything. The Third World you're talking about has hardly any industry and if we who do have industry can't buy oil we can't produce anything. And if we don't produce anything we'll have nothing to sell to the Third World to help them build up their industry. Nor would we be able to buy their goods or give them any credit or aid.'

'We're robbing them, we're exploiting them. This is a war against imperialism as well as a fight for our own survival.'

'You're at war with the world, that's your trouble.'

Marlowe pushed the petition away but the man next to him signed and passed it on. Marlowe watched, then continued more irritably than before. 'Anyway, all this talk about the so-called Third World is ridiculous. There's only one world and it contains rich, less rich, poor, very poor and starving. You can also find the same categories in many so-called Third World countries. "So-called" . because to say a country is part of the Third World simply means it is given money by other countries. It may be comparatively rich and well-organized like Singapore or Taiwan or it may be hopeless like India or almost any African country. And what about the first and the second worlds? No one ever mentions them. Who even knows what the first world would be?'

'Switzerland, California and All Souls,' said Tim, pushing the paper to Robert.

The others laughed. Orpwood watched the paper arrive in front of Robert.

'Robert?'

Robert shook his head.

Orpwood laughed abruptly and nervously. 'You'd risk nuclear war rather than stop interfering with other countries and maybe going without a few luxury goods?'

'The only way to put an end to war is to put an end to people.'

'Don't you care about being blown up, annihilated?'

Robert smiled. 'Not much.'

Orpwood smiled back briefly, then got up and moved on to other tables where his thin bent figure bobbed, pleaded and exhorted.

Tim turned to Robert. 'Many a true word.'

'Who says I was jesting?'

19

'Would you really not mind?'

'Probably. But I might not. Would you?'

Tim lifted his hands, palms upward.

High Table was still on the main course when the low tables began to drift away. The Fellows argued that to live in college throughout the year and to eat the same food as the undergraduates who were there for only twenty-four weeks would be insupportable. They also paid more for it. Tim was looking again in their direction.

'Are you going to wait for her?' asked Robert.

'No.' Tim did not move. 'I'm thinking of a gesture. Something unreasonable.'

'What for?'

'Just to make a gesture.'

The wine waiter, Harold, had been busy that evening supplying beer for the sconcing. He laughed when Tim asked him to deliver a bottle of champagne anonymously to the girl on the High Table.

'So long as you don't mind signing for it.'

'I'll sign. Make it the most expensive. What do you have?'

'There's only one sort and I can't remember what it is, but it'll cost you an arm and a leg.'

'Just let me sign.'

The bottle was delivered on a round silver tray. Tim was too far from High Table to see what it was. He and Robert left their bench and lingered inconspicuously amongst a crowd of gowned figures by the door. Suzanne seemed embarrassed and amused. Three times she put her hand to her black hair. The dons near her laughed and looked round. The Chaplain smiled and looked at the group near the door.

They went to Tim's room for coffee. With him it was a ritual that took precedence over conversation. He had an array of laboratory apparatus for making it but his favourite method was to grind the beans by hand, then use a tall china jug with a lid and plunger. He bought the beans in the covered market and blended them himself.

20

Thorough grinding and the pushing of the plunger were the most important parts of the ritual. Both had to be done very slowly. Before the plunger was pushed the full jug had to stand for several minutes, in winter in front of the gas fire.

Robert sat in the other armchair and used the small wooden grinder. It was a pleasant, undemanding activity. He never attempted to elevate it to the level of religious ritual attained by Tim nor did he bring to the pushing of the plunger the air of sexual solemnity. Tim's room was in almost every respect the opposite of Robert's: heavily and expensively furnished with lavish attention to detail, and altered almost daily. The damask velvet curtains had been made especially and were never opened fully, an antique brass table lamp was on throughout the day; respectable-looking volumes rested unopened in a glass-fronted bookcase. The table lamp had been lowered to the floor so that the room was cosily and inadequately lit.

'Music?' Tim asked but Robert shook his head. 'I suppose you're right. Must do something for Schools. Have you got a rehearsal tonight?' Robert nodded. 'You're out of your mind, doing a play in your final term.'

'One reason for not working.'

'How's it going?'

'Patchy. The theme is stated but is not present. Not felt.'

'What theme?'

'You're not really interested.'

'Tell.'

'Sin is punished. Excess and want of judgement bring retribution. The whole thing drips with irony. I have a vision of how it should be but it's a flickering vision and I'm not putting it across.'

'So it can't have life until you've imagined it?'

'Too much philosophy makes men mad.' Robert tossed the coffee grinder into Tim's lap and watched as the ritual was silently completed. When the coffee was safely in the cups he said, 'So what next?'

'Go and see her again, I suppose.'

'But she's already said she doesn't want to see you until after Schools.'

'She also said she wasn't going to go out at all and was going to work all the time, but she was there tonight.'

'The champagne will have annoyed her.'

'Think so?' Despite the off-handedness of his manner, talking about her made Tim's stomach contract and his neck and shoulder muscles stiffen. Robert was sensitive but in an aggressive way; either he took no interest or he was remorseless. He asked questions with a directness that made Tim wince, yet left him unable not to reply. Tim's attempts to retaliate fell flat because Robert seemed to answer as if he were not talking about himself. Tim tried nevertheless. 'And Mrs Barry?'

'Fine.'

'That's twice this week you've seen her.'

'It's easier the more pregnant she is.'

'Dr Barry doesn't mind?'

'Doesn't seem to.'

'Doesn't give a damn, maybe. The bursar's secretary gave him a lift again recently.'

'That doesn't mean anything.' Robert was aware of sounding more forceful than he'd intended.

Tim smiled. 'Like you and Anne, perhaps.'

'Perhaps.'

There was a knock at the door which Tim answered laconically. It was Hansford, a former school fellow who lived on the floor below. He and Tim had been in different houses at school and had hardly known each other but once at Oxford Hansford seemed to feel it important to maintain relations. He was something of a comic figure, very large and red-faced, with a voice that carried across two quads. Tim treated him with an amused tolerance which Hansford interpreted as friendship.

'Got any milk, Tim?'

'Plenty. Come in.'

Hansford nearly tripped on the light flex. 'God, it's dark

in here.' He opened the curtain slightly. 'Sorry, my eyes aren't up to much in the dark. Haven't seen you for ages, Robert. Been away?'

'No, I've been around. Nocturnally, anyway.'

'Working hard?'

'No.'

'Glad to hear it. I am, you see, so I'm encouraging other people not to. I reckon if I really push it, really screw myself to the desk, I should get a third. What do you think of that, eh?' He laughed abruptly.

'You're putting it that high?'

Hansford sat heavily on the table. 'I mean, I've got no illusions about the old grey matter. I was at the wrong end of the queue when they dished it out. Jolly lucky to be here at all, really, and if I leave with a degree I'll be the first in my family that has.' He laughed again and his red cheeks shook.

They talked about Schools until Robert, becoming restless, changed the subject by asking Hansford what he wanted to do when he went down. Hansford talked for some minutes about law and accountancy before asking what they intended.

'Travel round America,' Tim said promptly. In fact, he had made no such decision but had found that people usually regarded this as enough of an occupation not to ask any more.

'Haven't thought about it,' said Robert.

'Not going into the Church?'

Robert waved his hand from side to side as if he were still considering.

Tim produced milk and Hansford got up to go. He was so large he seemed to threaten the proportions of the room. 'Did you see that little creep Orpwood with his petition in hall tonight? I'm going to speak to the Dean about it. He should have been kicked out. I don't think Mr Farrow realized what was going on or he would have told the Dean himself.' Hansford belonged to a right-wing organization formed to counter what it saw as a threat to

23

the university from the far Left. His and Orpwood's dislike for each other was particularly personal, perhaps because they were from the same college. 'Nasty little creep, isn't he? Those bulging eyes. Vicious, don't you think?'

'He's all right when he's not evangelizing, when you get him alone,' said Robert.

'Mad, I reckon. Dangerous. You should see him at demos.' Hansford straightened his cravat in the mirror and tugged at his shirt collar where it was caught inside his jacket. 'What about the Ruskies walking all over the Middle East, then? Are we going to stand up to them, d'you think? Somebody will have to sometime. They'll be swarming over Christ Church Meadow next.'

'Look's bad,' said Tim, who paid no attention at all to news.

'But I reckon they'll back down when it comes to the crunch. They don't want to go to war. They're frightened of America.' He put down the milk and pulled with both hands at his collar. 'Bloody thing always gets caught. Anyway, we should let 'em have it if they want it. As long as we believe we will they'll believe it too and that's the best form of deterrence.' He picked up the milk again. 'Many thanks, Tim. I'll repay you tomorrow. Cheers. Bye, Robert.'

The room was quiet again. 'What time is your rehearsal?'

'Fifteen minutes ago. In Lincoln.' Robert stood.

'Drop by for a drink when you're back. I'll be up.'

'I'll look for the light.'

'No need. I'll be up. Won't be doing anything.'

The play was Middleton's and Rowley's *The Changeling*. Robert was directing it for the college drama society and had chosen it, he said, because it was dark, difficult and intense. Pressed, he would become evasive and facetious and say that, having none of those qualities himself, he sought them elsewhere.

In part, it was an attempt to fill the gap left by Anne but was already in this respect a failure. Although it took up most of his time, she still dominated his thoughts. When people told him he was committing academic suicide he would run his hand through his hair, nod, and ask them about their own work. Of his own, he said nothing. He did just enough to get through his twice-weekly tutorials. He attended no lectures, was not seen in Chapel and no longer spoke of going on to theological college. It was as if something within him had stopped and he was simply coasting, though he had become more energetic and active in apparently disparate ways.

There was a cast of twenty in *The Changeling* including servants and madmen, and it was to go on in the Newman Rooms, a large hall opposite Christ Church, often hired out for plays. The problems were endless: the publicity budget alone was now greater than the entire budget of any other play Robert had directed; the set had had to be redesigned; the designer had disappeared and there was talk of nervous collapse in Newport; the lighting firm had double-booked and its replacement was half again as expensive; one of the main characters had developed glandular fever and his substitute was barely adequate; the wardrobe mistress had hired lavishly from the Bristol Old Vic rather than from the local costumier; the madhouse scenes and the entire sub-plot were — as Michael Mann had warned — under-rehearsed and out of control. Finally, the publicity man had illegally stuck a poster on Wadham College door which had resulted in Robert receiving a formal summons from someone called the University Marshal. He had sent the publicity man instead who, wearing cap and gown, had had to apologize and submit to a fine. There was now an argument as to whether the drama society should pay it for him.

Most urgent, though, was the relationship between the two central characters, Beatrice and De Flores. The play stood or fell by this. Robert believed — at least, often said — that great drama consisted in the creation of great moments, that scenes should be built around those that contained the play's essence. So far the great moments were either being missed or were embarrassingly gauche. Yet they were essential. What Beatrice loathed in De Flores was what she saw of herself in him, and this he used to bind her closer. The idea appealed strongly to Robert, but he could not make it work.

That night's rehearsal was in a dark-panelled room which they were able to book easily because all but one of the madmen were at Lincoln. It was L-shaped and had a raised floor at one end so that when the chairs and tables were pushed back there was just enough room to act on the raised part. The oak panelling, lit but not illuminated by wall lamps, suited the play well.

People in Oxford were usually unpunctual and none but those who did not learn the habit was ever inconvenienced. When Robert arrived only Alsemero and De Flores were present. De Flores was played by an historian from Worcester called Malcolm who had done well as Mirabel in *The Way of the World* the previous term. Robert had cast him on the strength of that, ignoring a poor audition, and had so far admitted his mistake to no one. From the first rehearsal there had been something irritatingly light-weight about Malcolm. He lacked the surpressed, brooding, dangerous quality essential for the part. De Flores's bitter and ironical self-awareness was reduced by Malcolm to a nervous, jaunty, self-obsessed pirouetting. He acted as if before a mirror and needed to be far more compelling to make his conquest of Beatrice credible.

Nor was it simply a matter of miscasting. Robert knew he had given Malcolm less attention than he needed. Instead, most of his energy was directed towards Gina, who played Beatrice. She was an exciting actress with a strong low voice and an emphasis and timing that were instinctive and sure. In herself she was abrupt, remote, difficult to know; but on stage she was fluent and malleable. When Robert demonstrated what he wanted

26

she responded with a mixture of proud refusal and implied acknowledgement, the grudging yielding which the play demanded. When she played opposite Malcolm, however, she was dull and mechanical, further shaking his already shaky confidence.

Robert had decided he had to improve De Flores that night — in fact, to make or break him. It was impossible not to enjoy the exercise of power and the temptation to take over Malcolm's part in rehearsals was almost too strong. He felt that if he indulged it he would deny the cast and the play any chance of independent life.

Fortunately, it was not a full rehearsal with the full cast. Diaphanta and Jasperino arrived, then three others, but there was still no sign of Gina. He did not suspect her of being deliberately late, as if it were the leading lady's prerogative, but he knew that not everyone would think so. She was respected but not universally popular.

For some time no one spoke. They all looked tired and lethargic. The play was nearly a full-time occupation, on top of which they had their normal quota of essays and tutorials. Only Robert faced Schools.

Malcolm pulled a silver pocket watch and chain from his jeans, pausing until everyone had noticed.

'Gina's as awkward off-stage as on it. Is it too much Stanislavsky or is she just making sure we all notice her?'

The remark was obviously prepared and no one responded. Very soon afterwards, with the unconscious aptness of timing that characterized nearly everything she did, Gina pushed open the door and walked in without closing it. She took a chair by the empty fireplace and lit a cigarette, as if she were alone. Robert deliberately did not look up from his notes.

Malcolm put away his watch and stretched himself, self-consciously examining his fingertips. 'Which bit are we doing?'

'All your major speeches,' said Robert.

'All mine? Why?'

'To get them right.'

27

'But we've got . . .'

'And everyone else will play the parts opposite you, reading if necessary, dead-pan. No acting, no expression. They'll sit in chairs and say their lines like robots. So you can act your heart out before them.'

There was a stir of interest. Malcolm looked to the others in bewildered appeal, then back to Robert. 'I don't see the point. It's no good dead-pan. There's nothing for me to bounce off, no spark. It'll be like acting before Stonehenge.'

'Exactly. All the life and spark will come from you. De Flores is the motive force in the play. Go right over the top and get used to it so that when everyone else is turning it on you'll still be predominant.'

'You don't need me, then,' said Gina.

'I do.' He realized he should have said 'we'. 'You can respond very flatly.'

'Anyone can do that. Doesn't matter who responds. I've got an essay to write for tomorrow. We could all respond flatly.'

'You more than anyone.'

They had spoken quietly without looking up. They glanced at each other, very quickly, and Robert continued to read his notes. Out of the corner of his eye he saw Gina stub out her cigarette in the fireplace and get up. He did not know whether she would stay or walk out. In a few words he had created a crisis that could be decisive for the whole production. It was easy. Although his heart was thumping against his ribs he felt as detached as if it didn't really matter at all.

Gina walked slowly to the chair on the raised floor. 'Let's get on with it, then.'

'I'll need a few minutes to warm up,' said Malcolm. Like many actors he put great stress on physical and mental preparation. He believed in exercising together and touching each other. Robert did not believe in it but permitted it. The cult of sincerity and empathy always irritated him though he had never asked himself why.

Acting was pretending. It required practice, drill, repetition. No one could rely on precise mental tuning or empathy for every performance. It was, he thought, self-deceit to claim identification with an imaginary character. To be convincing night after night required responses that were well-rehearsed, almost automatic. Sincerity was a luxury.

'No warm up.'

Malcolm was disbelieving. 'I can't do it cold. I can't go into it just like that.'

'You can. Try.'

'But just a few minutes by myself is all I need. It won't take long.'

'Try it. You'll surprise yourself. Do it in front of Gina alone to start with.'

He stared until Malcolm looked away. Getting people to do what they didn't want was usually a matter of insistence and repetition. Robert's determination to see De Flores as he would have him coincided now with a desire, so far unacknowledged, to impress Gina.

Malcolm started. He went through his first speech while Gina sat on the chair and responded with the indifference and lack of expression that characterized her social dealings with him. The spectacle of cruelty purged the cast of apathy. They lined the panelled walls and looked on in attentive silence.

At the end of his speech Malcolm turned to Robert. 'It's no good. It doesn't work — you can hear it doesn't.'

'Go on with the next one.'

Malcolm gabbled through it, started on the third, then stopped. He held up his hands. 'Look, this is pointless. I can't act in a vacuum. It's not possible.'

'You're being precious.'

'Oh, come on . . .'

'Try again.'

His lines lost timing and rhythm and he lacked all conviction. Despite Robert's frequent admonitions he scarcely glanced at Gina. The result was so bad that the

29

others stared at him as if he had some horrid and fascinating disease.

Robert no longer thought his plan would work but it was too late to change now. He had to go farther or give up altogether. As soon as the last speech was finished he told the others to form a semi-circle around Malcolm with their chairs and take it in turn to feed him his lines in the same expressionless way as Gina.

Malcolm folded his arms. 'I can't do it. You'd better find someone else for the part. You're just trying to humiliate me.'

Robert continued to stare at Malcolm but was no longer thinking of him. The production could fold then and there and everything else in the world would remain the same. It made no difference what he did. The thought made him bold. 'It will work, Malcolm,' he said quietly. 'You can do it. To prove it I'll make it even worse. Everyone will feed you the lines in unison so you'll be acting before a chorus. It will be awful but you must force yourself to dominate them. Make them respond to you, not you to them. You can do it. You will make it work.'

Malcolm still stood with his arms folded. He was near to tears but did not walk out, inhibited perhaps by the semi-circle that had formed around him. It occurred to Robert that some of the cast might object but they seemed cowed, or perhaps were secretly excited. Gina's expression was unaltered.

Malcolm began in a weak, brittle voice. Robert stopped him, told him to unfold his arms and slow down. He began again and again Robert stopped him. 'Stand in the middle. Face people when you're speaking.'

Malcolm started for the third time. His voice trembled now on the edge of tears but as he went on the tears became incipient rage. The rage sounded more petulant than angry but Robert was encouraged by it. Malcolm flinched each time the chorus chanted its lines but after ten minutes of stops and starts he acquired a desperation that bred something like conviction.

30

'You're doing it, you're nearly there,' said Robert, gently now. 'But the chorus is helping you because it's being carried along by you. Chorus, please keep all expression out of your voices.'

Malcolm was still upset but now he wanted to succeed. He breathed deeply, paused, then delivered his lines rapidly and loudly as if he were angry with the chorus. There was a power and presence absent from his previous deliveries. It was no longer normal, nervous, touchy Malcolm. He had discovered a new part of himself.

'That is De Flores,' Robert said at the end. 'You've got there. You've done it.' He exaggerated deliberately. Malcolm looked drained but was unprotesting and thoughtful, absorbed in his discovery.

The others were chastened by the spectacle. They rehearsed three short scenes, the acting crisp and sharp. Gina listened impassively to what Robert said and reproduced his directions exactly with no acknowledgement other than the doing of them. At the end she left without speaking, though without appearing deliberately to avoid speech. She conveyed hostility as she conveyed sexuality, something she was aware of but could not be bothered with.

Robert locked the panelled room and returned the key to the lodge. He was very tired but until now he had not let himself admit it. It was as if his brain were being shut down section by section, like street lights in a city. He stood outside the lodge trying to remember where he had left his bike. Now that he thought about it, however, he could not remember bringing it, nor the last time he had ridden it. There was a cricket fixture list on the notice board. Yes, he had played cricket recently against Oriel. They had gone to the King's Arms to celebrate victory by three wickets and he had drunk too much. He had then lent the bike to someone from Oriel who lived a long way out and there had been some arrangement about its return or about his picking it up somewhere. Probably he would remember later. He had not always been so forgetful.

'Are you thinking or dead?'

He realized with a start that the pale, smiling figure by the wall was Tim, and felt unreasonably defensive. 'What are you doing here?'

'On my way to St Hilda's.'

'You're going to see her?'

'That's the idea. Come with me.'

'You don't want me there.'

'I do. That's what I'm saying.'

It was easier to go along than to say no and make the effort to go to bed. They walked down the Turl and on to the High. There was a fine soft rain and the road reflected the headlights of passing cars. Robert clutched his vital marked script to his stomach.

'She isn't going to like you,' he said. 'She spends half her time telling you to keep away and you don't.'

'She spends the other half saying she wants to see me.'

'She might not even be in yet. She might still be swilling port in our own Senior Common Room with whoever invited her.'

Tim nodded slowly and grinned again. 'Exactly. I am horribly jealous so I have to know, even if I don't like it'.

'Wait till the morning. It's not so easy to be jealous in daylight.'

'It is. I can be jealous of anything and without limit. In fact, I am jealous of her hairbrush.' A Headington bus stopped outside Queen's and they waited while half a dozen people shuffled from the shelter of the wall like demoralized infantry. 'Think about it. She uses it every day, pulls it through her hair, picks it up, fondles it with careless familiarity, drops it on her dressing table, permits it to remain in her room at all times. She won't do any of those things with me. I've come very near to chucking it out of the window.'

'Might as well chuck yourself out if that's the state you're in.'

32

'One day I'll do one or the other. Depends how I feel.'

They paused on Magdalen Bridge to look into the river. The Cherwell was mesmeric and inviting. Robert felt heavy and faintly sick with tiredness.

'You don't want me there,' he said. 'She certainly won't.'

Tim spat carefully into the water. 'Don't want to go myself. That's why I asked you.'

'Why go at all?'

'To make something happen.' He grinned, humourlessly. 'Have a nice sleep.'

The atmosphere in women's colleges always made Tim feel keenly predatory. When he stopped outside her door, though, it was as if his stomach had left him. He could hear music, something classical and quiet, and it struck him for the first time that she might not be alone. He waited but heard no voices, then pushed open the door.

She was working at her desk. She wore a red silk dressing gown with wide sleeves pushed back to her elbows. Her black hair was loose and she looked tired.

He leaned against the wall with affected casualness. 'I'll go if it's too late.'

For a second or two she looked more tired, then she got up. 'I was going to stop anyway.' She took the kettle from the corner by the window and walked past him to fill it. The silk dressing gown clung to her body and he could feel her warmth as she passed. She gave him a brief dark look. He went to the cushioned bench by the window where he usually sat.

'I suppose you did it?' she asked.

He nodded.

She smiled, showing the gap in her teeth upon which he used to compliment her until discovering she didn't like it. 'So it's you I have to thank.'

'You don't have to.'

'You must have known how embarrassing it would be, in front of hundreds of men. Is that why you did it?'

33

'Probably.'

'I think Peter was a little resentful. He seemed to think it was directed at him in some way.'

So it was the Chaplain who had invited her. 'Not at all. I didn't know who'd invited you. I didn't know you were coming.'

'That was it, wasn't it? Revenge because I hadn't told you.'

He smiled. 'Something like that.'

'And did you also come into my room before I was up and tie my tights in a knot?'

'I came to wake you.'

'I'd rather you had. It was horrible finding my tights like that.' She sat at the desk and rolled her fountain pen backwards and forwards with the tip of her finger.

'How's your work?' he asked.

'Stale. I used to enjoy revising but it's gone on too long this time. I'm not thinking about it any more. What about yours?'

He shrugged.

'How do you revise for philosophy?' she continued. 'I mean, there's not much you have to read, is there?'

'Not as much as you have. You're supposed to do some reading and a lot of thinking.'

'Are you doing any of either?'

'Not really. None, actually.'

'And Robert's doing his play. I don't understand how you can both go around not caring.'

'We started by not letting ourselves. It's become easier.'

'I wish I could be as nonchalant.'

'You'll get your first instead.'

The kettle boiled. She poured for him then went to the bed, propping herself up with pillows and folding her legs beneath her.

'Aren't you having any?' he asked.

'It keeps me awake. I wish you wouldn't mention firsts. Everyone goes on and on about it and it makes me feel worse. I'm not going to get one. I've worked hard but I'm not brilliant, like David Long.'

'Is he?'

'I think so. He's certainly very high powered.'

'Brilliant' and 'high powered' featured frequently in her vocabulary, as did David Long, a classicist from Magdalen. Tim found him exasperatingly pleasant and intelligent but was not sure whether to regard him as a serious rival. Nor was he sure that she really thought so much less of herself than she merited. She had got a first in history prelims and had worked hard since.

'Why did Robert do theology when he's not going into the Church?'

'He's never actually said he's not going to. He just seems to have switched off. You'd better ask him your-self.' She mentioned Robert uncomfortably often.

She pulled at the tassels on the bedspread. 'I know someone who's going to a monastery. He's taking a vow of celibacy.'

She often spoke about monks and priests and the incur-ably sick, all the unattainables. Tim had at first tried to make himself one but had had to give up when she did not seek to attain him.

'Your monk friend?'

'He's not quite a monk yet but he soon will be. He's interesting. He's a man who has everything, very bright, very positive, tremendous energy, very attractive. Now he's giving it up — dedicating it, is how he puts it. He believes he's called by God. You don't believe in anything, do you?'

'I don't know what I believe.'

'That's the same as not believing or it's nonsense.' She folded her legs the other way. 'Anyway, if you believe the news we might all be dead next week. I don't suppose you mind much about that, either.'

'I mind dying. I don't know whether I mind being dead.'

35

'David Long is a pacifist. Would you ever consider that?'

'I could murder millions. Daily.'

She looked down quickly to hide her smile. He knew now which game they were playing. It was necessary to appear serious.

'Why do you keep coming to see me?' Her eyes were still lowered and her tone was dull and flat.

'I'm trying to make you want me.'

She sighed dramatically. 'Men are always so inept on the subject of emotions. They never make them interesting. They shovel them on you until you can't breathe and then get upset when you tell them to stop.'

He put down his cup and stood. 'I'll go then.'

'Please do.'

She did not look up as he passed the bed. 'I don't believe you even like me. Lock the door behind you.' Her eyes closed and her face creased in sudden laughter. She held up one bare arm. He took it, knelt quickly and kissed her on the lips. She continued laughing and he had to break off. Her lips still smiled but she looked hard into his eyes. 'The last bit's true. I don't believe you do like me.'

'I do.'

She ran her fingers through the hair on his neck. 'You do not.' He kissed her again. 'No,' she said a short a while later. 'That really was horrible, finding my tights this morning.'

'I was only seeing if you wanted to come to the May morning ceremony.'

'It was a horrible, sinister thing to do. It made me feel awful.'

He allowed her to push him slowly off the edge of the bed until he was sitting on the floor, the back of his head resting against her thigh where the red gown had come open. 'What can I do to convince you?' he asked.

'You don't have to do anything. Just stop trying.' She stroked his hair again. 'You look dreadfully tired.'

36

'I'm not that tired.'

'Well, I am. I don't suppose that had occurred to you.'

As usual, he let her talk him into giving up. Once he had given up it wasn't too bad; conversation was easier. It was getting to that point that was difficult.

The outside doors were locked when he left and he had to climb out of the first floor window next to the stairs and jump. It felt gratifyingly illicit. He crossed the lawn quickly and picked his way through the flower bed to the wall. Once over it he was soon on Magdalen Bridge, where again he indulged in a ritual pause.

It was raining harder now. The walk was solitary and soothing, long enough for a delicious and painful reconsideration of word and gesture. It was like having some incurable but not incapacitating disability which refused to claim him utterly but prevented him from giving himself wholly to anything else. He liked the comparison but as he reflected on it he wasn't sure whether it was his own or whether Robert had once said something similar about Anne. Nevertheless, he could smile about it. It mattered and it didn't, like everything. The rain beat hard on the slates and windows of his rooms that night and, despite the residue of restless excitement, he fell quickly asleep.

Chapter Three

One night in the JCR bar Robert had described Chetwynd as 'immensely' thin, and had been teased about it ever since. It had almost become a college convention to describe anything small as vastly small or immensely tiny. But Chetwynd was certainly very thin, more so even than Tim whom by the same token might have been described as 'largely' thin.

He was a mature student in his late thirties, jaunty and opinionated, with cropped hair and an angry jutting beard. He was a notorious eccentric, a popular subject of gossip and exaggeration. His eyes were sad and soft, though, which gave him a lugubrious look. He always wore a baggy pair of brown corduroys, claiming they were a rare variety called 'agricultural corduroy', and in his Lovat pipe he smoked a secret mixture of his own. He had published a volume of poetry and owned a ruined vicarage in Shropshire. Weeks would pass when he would see or speak to no one. He would be glimpsed like some latterday Scholar Gypsy, silent, withdrawn, evasive, then would burst into a three- or four-day storm of garrulous drunkeness, neither sleeping nor working. These storms had more than once brought him to the attention of the proctors. He read English, specializing in Anglo-Saxon.

Since normally he was either invisible or drunk no one knew him well, but Robert knew him better than most. In their first year they had had night-long conversations but now saw less of each other. Robert felt vaguely that this was his fault, though for no particular reason. At lunchtime on the day following the rehearsal in Lincoln they ran into each other, coming out of lectures at Trinity. Attendance was rare for either. For Robert, at least, it was a conscience-salving alternative to revision since no actual work was required but it felt like work. They went to the White Horse, a narrow pub squeezed between Trinity and Blackwells, possessing, Chetwynd said, a desirable barmaid.

'A great heifer of a woman. Bovine passivity. Thighs like pillars of marble. She could crush me and swallow me and think she had a little wind.'

'You like them big and strong?'

'And little and weak. It's this hot weather. I have a near-permanent erection. Can you believe that?'

'No.'

'It's true but sadly not at this moment.' His pipe jerked in his mouth.

They had steak pies and beans, normal fare for both. Robert shook his head when Chetwynd bought two pints of draught Guinness to the table.

'I can't take this stuff at lunchtime. It knocks me out all afternoon.'

'Peace and oblivion — why worry? The first papers will be a day nearer and we'll be incapable of caring. Lesson here in how to prepare oneself for death.'

The sun came in through the small window. The Guinness was heavy and solid with the right amount and consistency of froth. Dust particles toiled in the sunbeams. Chetwynd looked round the bar which was beginning to fill with other undergraduates, most of them drinking halves. 'She's not here. Grazing peacefully with her bull somewhere.'

'You working?'

'Don't be obscene.' Chetwynd wiped the froth from his moustache. 'Woke up drunk yesterday evening in Balliol JCR. Christ knows how I got there. Hateful people, appalling buildings. Everyone serious and political.'

'I thought you were political.'

'Oh, I am, I am, more than any of them. But I recognize

the futility of it. There isn't going to be a revolution. No one wants it. No one. Not even the revolutionaries. They like the idea, the romantic appeal and they'd love the power, simply love it; but they'd be horrified if it actually happened because then they'd have to go on with it, and on and on and on. It wouldn't be a revolution any more. And then they'd be dead, victims of the tyranny to come. I used to be a card-carrying member of the Communist Party of Great Britain. Did you know that? Looking for my Spanish Civil War when there wasn't one. Now the only reasons I would go to Spain are sun, wine, women and boys. Though I'm no longer sure about the last.'

'Didn't know you were interested.'

Chetwynd arched his eyebrows. He talked so rapidly and with such fervour, whatever the subject, that it was hard to tell whether he meant all of what he said or none. There were no variations, no degrees of seriousness. 'My dear, you know nothing. Until I was twenty-five I was a virgin who thought himself homosexual and wanted to be a priest. Now that I'm no longer a virgin and no longer religious I no longer think I'm homosexual. Is that progress, I wonder? Have you ever been tempted?'

'I don't fancy men.'

'You lack imagination. Mind you, I'm annoyed by the way they've hijacked that pretty little word "gay". I can't use it in my poems without being misunderstood.' He grinned. 'Or understood. Ever my greatest fear.'

Robert resolved to leave in half an hour. He would have time to sleep it off and work on the play before his run.

'Then there's God.' Chetwynd held out his hand. 'Say nothing. I know it's your subject. I don't enquire whether or not you believe. It depends whether you have the necessary capacity for self-deceit.'

'Do you?'

'Not any more.'

Robert used to discuss religion with great enthusiasm but now he either avoided it or tried to discuss it in

40

relation to people other than himself. 'Why did you give up wanting to be a priest?'

'Mundane things like truth and evidence. I was keenly disappointed to find my nature fundamentally and finally empirical. I need reasons to believe and there is none, not a single good reason for believing in any of it. Most priests know that and it doesn't stop them, I admit, but in the end I just kept banging my head against a kind of integrity, if you can believe that of me.'

Robert smiled. 'I can, though I don't know why. You always do your best to undermine it.'

Chetwynd held up his hands. 'I had to acknowledge it because Christianity is so powerfully attractive. It would have seduced me utterly. It's wonderful. No tradition, no belief is worth so much as the little finger of Christ on the Cross. As an idea it's irresistible, but the more you look at its basis in fact — and it's on fact that it claims to base itself, is it not? — the less there is. It dwindles to nothing and you're left with faithless virtue: believe and it shall improve thee, act as if it is true and truly it shall seem so. You will at least be a better person and you may be granted life everlasting. Maybe. But . . .'

'Are you sure I haven't said all this to you?'

Chetwynd spread his hands over his thin face. 'Almost certainly. I have such a jackdaw mind. If I hear something I like I appropriate it immediately.' He smiled and his eyes glistened. 'I'll tell you what would make me believe. Something apocalyptic. If when I trickle out of here this afternoon the sun is blotted out and the sky becomes a great pair of lips and a mighty voice flattens me to the ground saying, "I AM", then would I worship. Willingly. But even so I know there'd be a malicious little corner of my heart that would thrill at the thought of all those mewling bishops and clerics having at last to take their own creeds literally. Truly should the righteous suffer.'

Robert drank. Chetwynd demanded little from his audience apart from attention and in that he demanded absolute fidelity. He remembered nearly everything he said. Next he spoke about thieving. He was an accomplished shoplifter and claimed to do it for the love of it rather than because he had any use for what he took. He hoarded some of what he stole and gave the rest away. Blackwells was his favourite target because they took the most stringent precautions. He boasted that in Hilary Term he had got away with two display copies of Williamson's *Guide to Tropical Diseases*.

'I stole a painting from Balliol JCR last night. It's back there now. Go and see if you can guess which — a test of how well you know me. Balliol louts were in there playing billiards so I had to edge it towards the door behind the chairs while their unappealing bums were thrust towards me. I had to pretend to be asleep in each chair all the way to the door. It took half an hour. It always astonishes me how unobservant people are.'

His Adam's apple jerked in his scrawny throat. 'Just got through the door with the painting under my arm when I met this drunken Marxist who started haranguing me. I dropped the painting and we went up to his room, clinging to each other and competing hoarsely in rhetoric. I pretended I was Polish. There was some Glenfiddich. I can take even the dialectic with that.' He put his chin to his chest and deepened his voice. 'I am for Marx. You English capitalist pig. "No, no," he protests, "I am for Marx too." Ees not possible for fascist hyena. Polish people do not drink. Filthy capitalist habit. Give me whisky. I look after.'

He moved his hands slowly across the table. 'Meanwhile, what do I find but his podgy little paw creeping up my thigh? I waited until it had nearly reached what I still call my private part then leapt to my feet crying, "Ees not Marx! Ees not Lenin! Only the hand of Marx for me!" Then I left, unsteady but intact for once.' He leant back and laughed loudly, attracting attention. His eyes watered. 'Of course,' he added between breaths, 'Balliol, you see. I should have known.'

Robert got more Guinness and they moved on to James

Joyce and Virginia Woolf. Chetwynd preferred Joyce because he could cope in literary terms with sex. Robert nodded, listened and wondered how many of his acquaintances Chetwynd would wear out during the next two days and night before sinking back into his Old English or Old Norse.

For some time there had been shouting and chanting in the street outside but the noise in the pub had made it indistinct. The shouting petered out and shortly afterwards the bar was filled by people carrying leaflets and placards. Orpwood was among them, his eyes shining as he expostulated with those near him. The placards denounced the American presence in the Gulf with such slogans as, 'Stop the Nuclear War' or 'Let's All Be Here Next Year'. They got between drinkers and their beer, were pressed against the ceiling or pushed to the floor until someone suggested stacking them outside and they were passed over heads to the door.

Orpwood spoke eagerly to a small girl with a deep frown and brown hair cut severely short. Robert had never met her but knew she was Janet Simpson from Somerville. She headed a Trotskyist group and several times interrupted Orpwood with sharp questions, apparently about what had happened outside.

'I fantasise about that woman,' said Chetwynd. 'Hard to believe when I look at her but when I can't I imagine lurking behind a curtain when she's addressing a meeting, then leaping like a stoat upon her and ravishing her to tumultuous applause. Bet she goes like a rabbit. That's not a political statement, though I don't doubt that's how she'd see it.'

Robert accepted a pamphlet from a girl in a pink tracksuit. It urged American withdrawal from the Middle East in order not to provoke the Russians, who were there already. There were paragraphs about economic imperialism, and the abuse of sovereignty and an announcement that the Iraqi ambassador was soon to speak at the Oxford Union.

Janet Simpson finished talking to Orpwood and he squeezed through the crowd to their table. He clutched half a pint and laid the other hand on Robert's shoulder. 'I borrowed some paper from your room this morning. Thought you were in because the door was open. I'll repay you but I had to finish an essay before the demo. Hope that was okay.'

'Fine. It's always open.' Robert never locked his door, which anyway opened by itself when the wind was westerly.

'Would you take me to your leader?' Chetwynd asked politely.

Orpwood was immediately wary, which was most people's reaction to Chetwynd. 'Who do you mean?'

'That woman.'

'Jan? You want to meet her?'

'At least that.'

Orpwood did not wait for Chetwynd but went off and brought Jan back to their table. She looked quick, intelligent and hard. Undergraduate life had not deprived Robert of all his natural courtesy and he offered her his seat.

'I don't want that.'

'Are you sure? I'm up now.'

'You don't have to patronize me.'

'I wasn't.'

She nodded at Orpwood. 'Why didn't you offer it to him, then?'

Robert shrugged and sat, trying to mask his resentment with a show of indifference.

Chetwynd grinned. 'You may have embarrassed my friend but you won't embarrass me. Please remain where you are.'

'What do you want?'

'I want you to convert me.'

'To what?'

'To your cause. What else? I am so pleased to see the Trots and Marxist-Leninists coming together, so glad the

44

ice axe is buried at last. The popularity of that tactic has always been a problem for my bourgeois conscience, you see, but now that you're reconciled I feel very much better. So please convert me.'

'Are you taking the piss?'

Chetwynd looked at his most lugubrious. 'I assure you I am not. I want you to tell me why you are opposed to nuclear war. That's a serious matter, surely?'

Janet stared at him hard but he neither smiled nor looked away. 'Isn't it obvious?' she asked at last. 'Most people are.'

'It's not at all obvious to me why anyone should wish to prolong the human tragedy, especially now we can all fry ourselves together. I'd like to be fried with you, by the way.'

'You are taking the piss.'

'I'm waiting for an answer.'

'Ask someone else.' She glanced at Orpwood and moved away.

Orpwood was indecisive. He made to follow but Chetwynd took his arm. 'No hard feelings. Sit and talk. I need some good talk.'

There was no malice in Orpwood. He liked to get on with people and talked as naturally as he breathed. They shifted someone's kitbag from the window seat and he squeezed in. The bar was now so crowded that those standing hardly had room to raise their elbows.

Orpwood was keen to talk about what had happened. 'We were going to occupy the Sheldonian and hold it till they got the pigs in to boot us out. We had loudspeakers and placards and posters and stuff. The idea was to draw attention to what's going on in the Middle East, maybe even get on the national news.'

Robert was irritated with himself for still being resentful of Jan Simpson. 'Who needs their attention drawn to it? It seems to me no one talks about anything else these days.'

'Well, it's more than just drawing attention. We've got

45

to persuade people to press for a sensible solution, to make their demands heard. I mean, maybe they don't want to go to war over who pinches whose oil. Or, even if they do, they're not being given any choice. I mean, do the people of this country really want to risk nuclear war so that the American government can appease its Jewish lobby?'

Chetwynd slapped his hand triumphantly on the table. 'Anti-semitism! The Left always is in the end, always. Despite its origins, its Jewish prophets, its proclaimed internationalism — in the end they always go for the Jews.'

'It's not that, it's not that at all,' protested Orpwood. 'I'm Jewish, my mother's family came from Hungary and they were all killed by the Nazis.'

'Exactly what I was saying. The Nazis — the left-wing National Socialist Workers' Party — killed your family. And if they hadn't Stalin would have. After the revolution they'll start on you. I'm serious. The left has to have enemies and the Jews are naturals. I daresay you still think all men are brothers beneath the skin, not beasts. Am I right? Go on.'

Orpwood's eyes shone with sincerity. 'Look, my movement is not anti-semitic. We oppose the aggression of the State of Israel but that's a different matter. So do many Israelis.'

Robert hated the emotion generated by a political argument. 'What happened when you tried to take the Sheldonian?' he asked.

Orpwood continued staring, almost pleadingly, until Chetwynd grinned, and he turned to Robert. 'They were ready for us. We didn't get in. It was guarded by pigs and proctors. There were even some bulldogs in bowler hats. Amazing — I didn't realize they still went in for all that. I mean, we could have had a punch-up there and then but we decided to save it. Someone must have talked. Jan reckons there's a Special Branch spy in the group. She wants him rooted out and dealt with.'

'Dealt with?' asked Chetwynd.

'Well, it depends. Personally, I think it's more likely to have been loose talk overheard by fascists like Hansford and his mob.'

'Mad Hansford should be dealt with, of course.'

'That's what Jan thinks.'

'I'm sure she does. But it's not because of his politics that I think so. It's because he's Hansford.'

'He's not so bad,' said Robert. 'He's friendly enough. Helpful.'

Chetwynd raised his eyebrows. 'So were all the great dictators, in their ways. Fond of dogs, loving fathers, keen amateur historians to a man.'

'Very true,' said Orpwood.

'Of whom I'm passionately jealous. Jealous of every last one.'

'Jealous?'

'Of course. If you can't be William Shakespeare — I was thirty-one before I acknowledged I couldn't — you have to be dictator of the world. It's the only acceptable alternative. Power is so attractive.'

Orpwood took it seriously. By the time Robert left the two men had ordered more beer and were arguing about Lenin. Near the door Jan Simpson and some of her supporters were in intense conversation. They talked in low voices and stopped while Robert passed them.

It was absurd to feel so drunk on two pints, he told himself. The sun made it worse. He would go back, sleep, have tea, go for a run, get on with the play. Another day without work.

On the other side of the Broad he saw Suzanne and a man he did not know looking in the window of Thornton's second-hand book shop. He crossed with a vague notion that by talking to her he would be doing Tim a favour. As he did so he glimpsed the Daimler Majestic he had seen when walking with Anne. He would find out who owned it, perhaps put a note on the windscreen, make an offer. He approached Suzanne with renewed enthusiasm.

'Looking at the covers won't help. You've got to open them. I keep telling Tim that.'

She was nervously lively. 'Robert, you're always creeping up on people. I never see you first.'

'That's because I'm so drunk I can only come at you sideways.'

'You're not that drunk.'

'Sort of.'

She introduced the man as David Long, the classicist she so often mentioned to Tim. He was thick-set and had cheerful, open features. His manner was frank and perceptive. In Robert's experience there were two kinds of classicists, the mad and the disconcertingly sane. They were all intelligent. David was one of the sane. 'At least you can enjoy being drunk,' he said with a smile. 'And you're not so drunk you won't be able to enjoy being sober again.'

'I think he's just proud to be drunk so early in the day,' said Suzanne.

Robert smiled. 'Not proud. Just postponing the decision whether to work or sleep, though I know already which I'll choose.'

Suzanne spun on her heel in exasperation. 'Why must everyone talk about work the whole time? It's bad enough doing it without having to hear about it everywhere you go. It's like some dreadful disease we've all got and all we want to hear of is someone in a worse state than ourselves.'

'It's either work, warm weather or war,' said David. 'Though I think war's becoming rather declassé.'

'I'd sooner talk about the weather, it's so beautiful,' said Suzanne. 'I love the heat. It's awful having to be inside all the time.'

Robert tried to see her as Tim might. Her face was pretty but changeable, a provocative, inconstant face. He could see that you might not know where you were with her. At the same time, she looked as if she would readily be tender and affectionate. The gap between her teeth was beguiling, her black hair striking. 'Take comfort from one of the two worst cases. I'm doing no more work than Tim.'

She looked archly at him. 'But, Robert, I always feel better for talking to you, anyway.'

David Long laughed and turned away.

'Tim tells me you work all the time,' Robert continued, watching her carefully.

She stopped smiling. 'If Tim had his way I wouldn't be fit to sit a single paper. Is he really not doing any work?'

'None that I know of.'

'Well, he must. Make him.'

'I'll tell him you said so.'

She turned to join David. 'Don't say that or he never will.'

The next few days grew even hotter, and it was the Chaplain's suggestion that he and Robert held their next tutorial afloat. They took one of the college punts. Robert punted in uneasy silence while the Chaplain reclined in the stern reading Robert's essay.

Afterwards, the Chaplain let the sheets of densely written paper slip through his fingers on to the slats in the bottom of the punt. His other hand trailed in the water and he gazed at the river bank as it passed in slow time with Robert's punting. The Chaplain was almost impossibly handsome, slender with an intelligent sensitive face and very blonde hair. His smile was disarmingly and misleadingly shy.

'It's not the existential crises, the dark nights of the soul that are the problem,' he said. 'There's no danger of not noticing them. In any case, they represent a spiritual progression, or are supposed to. It's everyday life, tomorrow and tomorrow and tomorrow, which is the real enemy. All the mundanities of which our lives are made up, not special, not noticeably evil. Apathy, habits of

49

thinking, habits of feeling, normality. The most dangerous devil is the noonday devil. He makes it seem as if nothing matters. You might do evil because you want to or because it's wicked or just because it's different but it doesn't matter anyway. Nothing matters. He robs life of all value, and because you're shamed and frightened by that you start to hate yourself, which makes you hate others. You harden your heart and despair, the sin that cannot be forgiven. You hate God. And habit is this devil's friend. Habit is particularly powerful, it's what keeps many people going. But we've been through all this before.'

He picked up Robert's essay and looked again at the flimsy sheets, holding them as if about to let them float away. 'What you seem to be arguing is that, leaving aside the physical ills of the world, evil is that with which people wrestle in spiritual crises. It may be of supreme importance to them but it remains a purely private affair: you have it and I don't and there's an end to it. We are not in the same boat, as it were.' He smiled. 'You make it sound like an haphazard and self-centred drama, incapable of generalization, without serious effect or consequence. You seem to be trying to chip away the reality of evil.'

Robert had written the essay three nights previously in the early hours following a day of rehearsals. It was, he suspected, a torrid, thoughtless outpouring in which he had striven to convince by intensity rather than by argument. He could barely recall what he had written and it struck him now that in one sense the essay resembled his bicycle: he remembered only that there was one. 'I hope that's an oversimplification of what I wrote.'

'Simplified in order to provoke. It would be much more useful to discuss how you should prepare for your doctrine paper; but since nothing I can say now will make you work when you seem more interested in other things, that's by the by. The reality or not of evil is irrelevant for

50

Schools, of course, but as you raised it I thought perhaps you might concede it has some importance.'

'I'm not quite the sceptic you make me out.'

'It's not me that makes you out to be one.'

The sun glinted and flashed on the Cherwell. From the park on one side came the smell of mown grass and from the fields on the other the incessant chirping of crickets and the occasional swish of cow's tails amidst swarms of flies. Robert, stripped to the waist, crouched to avoid an overhanging willow. One of the few who had done no sunbathing that term, his skin was dazzlingly white. He enjoyed feeling the sweat run freely from under his arms as at the end of each push he trailed the pole as a rudder.

'You'll get sunburnt,' the Chaplain said quietly. 'You really will. It's very hot.'

'I think I enjoy being careless.'

'Is that why you're not working?' Robert performed an elaborate manoeuvre with the pole, on which he pretended to concentrate wholly but the Chaplain continued quickly. 'It's not that, is it? Nor is it that you're just not bothered, like your friend Tim, nor because of your play nor anything else like that. I think it's some-thing deeper. I think you've stopped working because you've stopped believing.'

Robert let the pole slip through his hands back into the water.

'Is there anything you actually want to talk about?' asked the Chaplain.

Robert leaned on the pole. He didn't want to have to talk at all. 'What is sin?'

The Chaplain lifted his dripping fingers from the water, looked at them and put them back again. 'Wilful absence from God. A turning away, an assertion of self, a denial of dependence, hence ultimately a denial of our real selves and of Him.'

'If there were no one to turn away, then sin could not exist?'

51

'Unless as an hypothesis in the mind of God, if you want to speak of it that way.'

'Is evil negation, then?'

'Yes, but not in the sense you want it to be. Not a dramatic, denying gesture, exciting and attractive. Evil is not interesting. It's pervasive, undramatic, shabby, real. A condition of life, unnoticed, unremarked. Its most common manifestation is indifference. That is the deepest and most lasting cruelty.' He lifted his fingers again, this time with a wide sweep that sent a line of drops across Robert's body. 'What have you done with that form?'

'I've got it, it's on my desk.' The application form for theological college should have been in by the start of the year.

'Fortunately, they've got spare places. They usually have these days. But they won't hold them open much longer. They're closing very soon.'

Two other punts at the bend were filled with boisterous parties who had wine and straw hats and were trying to ram each other. Robert steered around them, then drifted down the reach beyond Parsons Pleasure.

'Supposing someone believes in God, in the reality of sin and evil, the whole thing, but is indifferent to it, shrugs his shoulders. What difference would that make to anything?'

The Chaplain smiled. 'I'd say he was making a pose of indifference.' He looked again at the river bank. 'But the difference is the difference it makes to you. The more you deny, the less you are. In diminishing yourself you diminish everything. The urge to diminish comes from pride and fear. You fear belief because of the challenge it brings with it and you are too proud to humble yourself. For you there are no other reasons. Evidence for or against the existence of God is irrelevant to you, though useful as an excuse. Then when very occasionally a sense of evil, of your own sin and denial, forces itself through the crusted rock of your daily life, you dramatize it and pretend it's something it isn't. You make it a crisis, something dramatic and extraordinary. In fact, it's common-place and real, but you don't take the real seriously, perhaps because it is so commonplace. You cease to care, you don't take your own life seriously, and that's when the noonday devil comes for you. He takes you seriously.'

Robert leaned on the pole and the punt surged through the water. The Chaplain was smiling again but looking carefully at Robert. 'How's Anne Barry?' he asked.

'Very well, I think.'

'Is she happily married?'

'I don't know.'

'I hope she is.'

Parsons Pleasure was an area of grass fenced off on all but the river side by green corrugated iron. It was a place for male dons and undergraduates to bathe naked and was the subject of many tales and jokes, mainly concerning bathers' reactions to punt-loads of women. These were supposed to go round the far side of an inter-vening island but rarely did.

This time there was a dozen or so bathers, all lying on the grass except one: a tall, pot-bellied don who stood on the bank facing the river. He wore black shoes and black socks held up by black suspenders just below his knees. He carried a black briefcase and stared belligerently at the punt, turning to face it as it passed. His skin was as white as Robert's. His belly bulged obscenely over an obscenely long penis.

The Chaplain gazed indolently back at him. 'Do you think he's trying to tell us something?'

'I don't think he likes us. Unless it's that he's pleased with himself.'

'Perhaps he thinks he can help if we lose the pole.'

They negotiated the weir, sliding the punt down on rollers at one side, and continued downstream towards Magdalen Bridge. 'Aren't we committing what you're condemning me for?' asked Robert. 'Discussing the nature of sin and the reality of evil whilst punting in Oxford on a hot afternoon. It's a way of making the subject attractive. And potentially dramatic.'

'It's an acceptable way to be serious.'

'And what conclusions have we reached?'

'Your sin is denial but you relish it and will do nothing about it.'

'Do you have a sin you relish?'

The Chaplain shielded his eyes against the glare with one slim brown arm. 'Yes, but I pray not to.'

Robert felt he had won a small victory. 'What do you mean by prayer?'

'The attempt to open yourself to God and consciously to experience your relationship with Him, which is ultimately your life.' The Chaplain spoke carelessly and again dangled his hand in the water. 'Look, shall we turn round? This is useless as far as Schools are concerned. It's nearly tea-time and I'd like to punt.'

Back in his room thoughts of Anne Barry, Schools and *The Changeling* gathered around Robert like old familiars. There was never any progression in his thoughts about Anne, just the repetition characteristic of obsession. Thinking of Schools was as futile as thinking of death: they were inevitable and universal and would be realized only in the personal, when it was too late. The play at least he could do something about, though, and he had begun making notes for the next rehearsal when Hansford knocked and opened the door unbidden. His big red face was redder than usual and he was out of breath. 'Do you know where Orpwood is?'

'No.'

Hansford shut the door and leaned against it. 'His room sounded empty when I came past but I heard Jan Simpson and some others had been around here plotting something.'

'I don't know, I haven't seen him.' Robert had no time for plots, real or imaginary.

Hansford did not notice Robert's irritation. 'It might

have concerned me, you see. You know they wanted to occupy the Sheldonian but couldn't because the police stopped them? It's all to do with this Iraqi geezer coming to speak at the Union. Now they're looking for scapegoats and saying it was me that tipped off the police.'

'Was it?'

'No, I didn't know anything about it. Otherwise it would have been, I don't mind admitting. The other reason they might be gunning for me is that we're going to hold a protest meeting when this Iraqi bloke comes.'

Hansford looked absurdly serious. Robert put down his notes wearily. 'Do you want some tea?'

'Love some, thanks.' Hansford sat heavily in the only armchair and wiped his face with a blue-and-white spotted handkerchief.

'No milk, I'm afraid.'

'It's all right, I can do without. Wouldn't put it past them to come to my room and duff me up.'

'Perhaps you should plan an escape route.'

'I've recce'd the window. It's sheer, no way down, not even a drainpipe.'

The difficulty in dealing with Hansford was that his absurdity and his good nature were in equal contention. Robert searched for the teabag he remembered having. 'Why not go up?'

'Eh?'

'You're on the floor below. There are ledges above all the windows. If you pull yourself up onto the one above yours you could climb into the passage outside Tim's room and hide in there.' Robert liked the sound of his own advice. It was decisive and easy, and anyway for someone else. 'If you couldn't get into his room or if you didn't want to go there you could go farther along the ledge and step over the next one around the corner and get in through my window. It's always open.'

Hansford looked impressed. 'Gosh, Robert, that could be the answer. How wide is this ledge?'

55

'Wide enough. Have a look. I climbed on to it when a shirt I was drying fell off the windowsill.'

Hansford got up from the armchair and looked. His wide body almost filled the window. 'Sure you don't mind?'

'Positive.'

'Robert, you're a real brick. You may have saved my life. You never know with this crowd.'

Hansford relaxed over tea. He told Robert the latest news of the Middle Eastern crisis and detailed the complement and armament of the American carrier force sent to counter the Soviet presence. He thought it an outrage that the apologist from the Iraqi embassy was permitted to roam the country disgorging propaganda. When he finally stood to go he said, 'Must get back to the grindstone. Haven't done my daily quota yet. Hope Orpwood's not in his room. Better be prepared if I'm going to meet him on the stairs.'

It was hard to imagine a confrontation between Hansford and the diminutive Orpwood. 'I don't think he's in. He's normally got music on if he is.'

'Good. Thanks for the tea and the tip. Hope I can do the same for you sometime.' His face shone with goodwill. 'How are all the angels and devils and whatever?'

'The what?'

'All the theological stuff. That's what you read, isn't it?'

'Ah, yes, well, still all there.'

'All mumbo-jumbo to me, I'm afraid. I mean, I go to church and all that but I can't pretend to understand. All a bit over my head. I need clever blokes like you to explain it to me.'

'I doubt that you do. Doesn't help to study it.'

'Too much of the pale cast of thought, I suppose?'

'Yes. But it's hard not to think.'

Robert saw him to the door and watched him go unmolested down the stairs.

Undergraduates were invited to drink sherry in the President's lodgings at least once a year. The idea was that the President should get to know them but he had in any case a formidable memory and rarely forgot anything he heard.

The usual difficulty of being natural over sherry meant that nearly everyone found the parties awkward. The dons were often reluctant and embarrassed, the under-graduates mainly gauche and tongue-tied. Those who were not fell easy prey to the President's anxious wife who hopped like a sparrow from group to group, confusing names, interrupting, repeating herself. Robert arrived late, following his run, in the hope that this would mean there was less time for discussing work.

The President was a brisk and tubby man with an iron-grey moustache. He was a well-known historian who in early middle age had taken holy orders and then resumed his academic career. He talked with disconcerting precision and fluency. When Robert arrived the President and Hansford were heavily engaged discussing the inter-national situation. He tried to move discreetly towards where the President's wife was talking about her garden to two botanists, but the President spotted him.

'Robert, how nice to see you. I was thinking only the other day that it was some time since I'd seen anything of you but then I concluded you must be locked in your room or in the library preparing for Schools. Was I right? Your first paper must be quite soon.'

Robert still occasionally began encounters with auth-ority by reverting almost to childhood, starting with a self-effacing grin and a non-committal remark which, when explanations were demanded, grew immediately into a monster of benality or self-contradiction.

'Well, off and on, yes.'

'What do you mean?'

'I mean I've been in my room or in the library some of the time but not all of it.'

The President finished his sherry. 'When is your first paper?'

57

'On the Thursday. Yes, Thursday.'

'That's the Old Testament, isn't it?'

'No, I believe it's doctrine.'

'I think you'll find it's the OT. In fact, I'm sure you will. But you'd better check very soon rather than take my word for it.'

Robert nodded. 'No, you're right. I remember now. The OT.'

Hansford interrupted with further views on the international situation. It had been reported in the press that morning that Libya and Iraq might have developed a nuclear weapon and were preparing to use it.

'That's another point all these CND types don't realize,' he said emphatically. 'Inevitably, the day will come when all the Gadhaffis and Amins and ayatollahs and madmen are going to have nuclear weapons. They'll get them eventually whatever we do about disarmament because the technology's all there now. Everyone knows it — you can't abolish knowledge. And when they have them they'll have no moral inhibitions about using them. They think it's a religious duty to carry out Allah's holy war, or whatever. The only thing that will stop them is the certainty of instant and overwhelming retaliation. Don't you think?'

They helped themselves to more sherry. Dr Barry joined them, flashing a quick conspiratorial smile at Robert. The President spoke about moderating influences within Islam. Robert looked at Dr Barry's small bird-like face and tried to imagine Anne making love with him.

'What do you think, Robert?' asked the President crisply.

'I'm sorry?'

'Leaving aside for one moment the immediate political and military consequences — including the possibility of nuclear annihilation, which seems a lot to leave on one side, I confess, but one has to make certain assumptions about survival if one is to discuss at all — leaving all that aside, what, I wonder, should be the Christian approach

58

to the problem of war? What should the good Christian do?'

The Chaplain joined them, looking bored. He glanced about as if not listening. 'Pray that the big bang will bring him closer to heaven.'

Dr Barry laughed and the President guffawed humourlessly. He and the Chaplain were said not to be in sympathy.

'I think it's a jolly difficult question,' said Hansford.

'But need it be a problem?' asked Dr Barry. 'There's surely enough in Christian teaching about justifiable war for the Christian to be able to select the bits that support his case. The wise Christian, that is.'

The President shook his head. 'But let us assume a Christian who is not wise in the self-serving sense that David no doubt has in mind. What should he do? Robert?'

'Pray for peace, I suppose.'

'At least that, I'd have thought. Is that all?'

'I don't know that there's much else he could do.'

'Prayer may involve other things,' the Chaplain said, off-handedly.

The President snorted. 'But what should they be? Should the Christian be a pacifist? There is a respectable case to be made for Christian pacifism. Or should he fight for what he believes is right? After all, is life the absolute value? Or, to put it another way, is death the greatest disaster that can befall the Christian — or anyone else? If not, would the Christian be justified in killing?'

'You have to fight for what you believe in,' said Hansford. 'No doubt about that.'

'Does that apply equally to the other side?'

'Oh yes,' Hansford nodded confidently. 'They may be as certain that they're right as we are that we're right. The difference is, we are.' There was a surprised silence until Hansford said something to the President about the cricket.

Dr Barry turned to Robert. 'You should come and see

Anne more often. She misses her old friends. Since she's married a don they tend to keep away.'

'I don't want to be in the way.'

'Don't worry about that.' There was again a hint of complicity in Dr Barry's smile. 'Come any time.'

The Chaplain raised his delicate eyebrows. 'You could discuss marriage and the Christian. That might even count as revision. Excuse me.' He moved off to talk to a fresh-faced newcomer.

When Robert left he was followed into the lobby by Hansford. They stopped by the umbrella stand, the smell of sherry heavy on Hansford's breath. 'Can you speak to Tim about that escape-route you were telling me about? When I described it to him he didn't seem to understand. Looked at me as if I was off my head. Didn't even seem to realize there was any threat from Orpwood and his crowd. Will you talk to him soon? You never know when I might have to use it. I'll probably go straight for your room anyway, but it would be nice to have Tim's in reserve.'

'I'll talk to him.' Something in Dr Barry's words, or his manner, had made Robert sad. He reacted by being care-less and flippant. 'Have you thought about a gun?'

'Thought a lot about that. I've got a twelve-bore at home but I don't know what the college view on guns is. Perhaps I should have a word with the President. What do you think?'

'Automatic?'

'Lord, no, The old man wouldn't have one on the place.'

'Orpwood armed?'

'Doubt it, but it's his friends I'm worried about. Look, you will talk to Tim soon, won't you? I want to get it sorted out.'

'I will, yes. Where would you keep it — the gun?'

'Under the bed, I suppose.'

'Not on your desk?'

'Might alarm people.'

'Maybe.'

'But it's really all right for me to use your room as a bolt-hole?'

'Anytime.' Robert turned away.

Chapter Four

It was the silly season, the most social time of the year. There were tea parties, lunch parties, drinks parties, punting parties, dinner parties, breakfast parties — and parties. College lawns sprouted new celebrants daily.

Michael Mann was celebrating his production of *A Midsummer Night's Dream*. Like his productions, his parties were lavish and subsidised by a wealthy father. He would have been most at home with a film set and one day, perhaps, would have one. Though he was notorious for his outbursts of bad temper and for reducing some of his cast to tears, people flocked to his parties and boasted of knowing him.

Both Robert and Tim were invited and each had at first told the other he wouldn't go, Robert because he was too busy and Tim because he liked to affect a disdain for social occasions. He admitted, though, that he hated not being invited. Eventually Robert decided he would have time because of a cancelled rehearsal and because he realised Anne would be there, possibly without Dr Barry. Tim changed his mind because Robert had and because Robert had pointed out that Suzanne too might be there. They went late, waiting until it was well underway.

Robert wore his usual T-shirt and jeans and had rushed dinner. Tim had missed dinner, as he often did, on the assumption that deprivation was good for him. He would then eat bowls of cereal and drink Earl Grey tea and whisky through the early hours. He wore cricket flannels, a maroon velvet jacket, a white shirt and bow tie and carried a straw boater. He neither played cricket nor ever once wore a hat, but enjoyed dressing as a period piece.

They walked together through the narrow streets. 'Enter gentleman and menial,' said Robert. 'I should be staggering behind with your trunk.'

'Nobody's even looked yet,' said Tim. 'The only way I get looked at is if I take my BMW everywhere.'

'It's an Oxford problem. So many people trying to be remarkable nobody pays any attention. You could walk naked and they wouldn't notice.'

'Some friend of Hansford's at Christ Church did that last term. Walked into the Bear. They didn't say anything until he asked for a drink, then they wouldn't serve him because they reckoned he must be under-age.'

'Did Hansford come back to you about his escape route?'

'Come back to me? He almost wiped me out. Went on about it for about forty minutes after I'd just got up. Off his head. I said he could walk in my door and out of my window whenever he liked. Just don't wake me, that's all. I went back to bed afterwards.'

The party was held on the lawn of New College cloisters. Laughter and the squeals of girls could be heard from some distance away. The cloisters were cool and dark and both men paused there, narrowing their eyes against the brightness and the vivid green of the lawn. Beneath a large bay tree stood trestle tables laden with drink. People clustered around them, many sitting on the grass, a few who had had papers that afternoon wearing subfusc. Most of the girls were in long summer dresses, with white the predominant colour. A record-player by the tree played some Mozart which Robert felt he probably should know, or perhaps did know.

Robert looked unsuccessfully for Anne. 'Can't see Suzanne,' he said.

'Nor me,' Tim moved his boater from one hand to the other, then held it behind his back. 'If we stand here long enough, though, everyone will see us.'

'Not sure I want that.'

Tim smiled, 'Me neither, all of a sudden. I hate entries. Anne's over there, half left.'

She was talking to another girl, a glass of orange juice held lightly in both hands on top of her stomach. She had her hair up and wore a black hat with a broad brim that curved down over her eyes. She smiled at Robert when she saw him and the other girl followed her gaze.

'Good hunting,' he said to Tim. He smiled back at Anne as he moved towards them, then found himself holding the smile for an inordinate time as he stepped around people and over legs and dresses.

Anne introduced the other girl as Jean.

'Pleased to meet you.' Robert extended his hand but she was not expecting it because few students shook hands, and he had half withdrawn it before she reacted.

They clasped clumsily and briefly. He indicated the sky with his hand, knocking her arm. 'Beautiful evening. Sorry.'

'Perfect. That's all right.'

Anne drank her orange juice.

'Looks like the world and his wife are here,' Robert continued.

Jean looked about her as if noticing for the first time. 'Yes, there are a lot. Are you an actor?'

'No. Not on stage, anyway.' He had to repeat it for her. She said she'd seen someone she had to speak to immediately, and moved off.

He addressed the brim of Anne's hat. 'Didn't mean to drive your friend away.'

She looked up. 'She's not my friend. We met on our first day in Oxford and have felt obliged to speak ever since. It's time we called a truce. I was just wondering how to get rid of her when you turned up. Now I know.'

'That hat looks good. Brings out your eyes.'

She touched it with the tip of one finger. 'I felt like a touch of flamboyance.'

Her mouth was more firmly compressed than usual,

stitched at the corners with a few tiny lines. Her eyes looked full as if something were pressing them from behind. 'Do you feel all right?' he asked.

'Perfectly all right.'

'You're drinking orange juice.'

'I like orange juice.'

Her manner was both hostile and demanding.

'David's not here, then,' he said, trying to sound matter-of-fact.

'He's over there.'

She indicated the far side of the lawn where Dr Barry sat with three actresses from *The Dream*. One had spread her long white dress like milk on the grass around her. She swayed with laughter at something Dr Barry was saying.

The silences of women engendered in Robert a strong urge to speak yet robbed him of any feeling for what to say. Anne stared at him without remission. 'Would you rather I went?' he asked at last. Her brown cheeks were smooth and hard. The brim of her hat cast a decisive shadow across her jaw. 'I'll go if you like.'

'I don't think you can ever have loved anyone,' she said slowly.

'What do you mean?'

Out of the corner of his eye he saw Tim talking to Suzanne and two other girls. Suzanne shook back her black hair then snatched Tim's boater from his hand and put it on her head. He witnessed the incident with the clarity and unreality of a vivid memory.

Anne smiled at the approach of Michael Mann. He stretched out his arms and bent to kiss her on both cheeks, arching himself so as not to touch her stomach. She winced and laughed as his beard touched her. 'You feel like a nest of spears.'

'I'll shave it off if you promise to let me do it every day.'

He turned to Robert with a confident smile. 'Nice to see you, Robert. How are rehearsals?'

65

'Nice to be here. Thank you. Slow and far to go.'

'You've got Schools coming up, haven't you?'

'Coming on quickly.'

'Hope I can be as calm as you next year. Are you not drinking?'

Robert had not realized he had no drink. 'No — yes, that is, but not yet.'

Michael laughed and laid his hand on Robert's shoulder. 'Over there on the table. Help yourself.'

'I shall.' Robert nodded. Anne was smiling now but avoiding his eyes. He was determined not to be dismissed. 'Congratulations on *The Dream*,' he said to Michael. 'A national success, not just an Oxford one.' The production had been favourably reviewed in *The Times* by an occasional drama critic who was known to be enthusiastic about the girl who played Titania.

Michael shook his head. 'Even so, it was never quite right. You know how it is, Anne — more orange juice?'

'No, thanks.'

'Robert — you sure?'

'In a minute.'

Michael raised his hands in mock despair and moved off. Robert looked at Anne. 'What do you mean?' Her face seemed to alter as he watched. The texture of her skin softened, her features became less sharp, her lips relaxed.

'Nothing. I was being selfish and silly. I'm annoyed with David, that's all.'

'But I want to know why you said it.'

'Robert, don't go on.'

'Why did you say it?'

She sighed and looked away. 'It's only for your own sake that you want to know.'

'Who's sake did you say it for, then?'

She was looking again to where Dr Barry still sat with the three girls. 'You've only ever been interested in yourself.'

66

He tried to sound understanding. 'Has David upset you?'

'You weren't interested in me or the baby.'

'I was, I am. You went off me.' It was simple, once said, but it felt brutal. He had never admitted it before. 'Anyway, you can't blame me for not being very interested in David's baby.'

She stared evenly back at him from beneath the hat. 'What makes you think it's David's?'

Tim appeared, clutching four empty glasses in the fingers of one hand. He greeted Anne with elaborately good-humoured courtesy, then turned to Robert with an expression of mock hopelessness.

'What do you do with a woman who won't have dinner with you, who says she's got to work, but has already drunk too much to concentrate?'

'Give her more,' said Robert.

Anne smiled at Tim. 'Better make sure it's more than you give yourself.' Without looking again at Robert she turned and walked over towards her husband. He saw her coming and got quickly to his feet.

'Trouble is, they're all making a big joke of it now,' Tim continued. 'Suzanne started out being much more friendly than I'd expected so I thought I'd push my luck a bit and suggest dinner and then she made me say it again and her friend heard and then the others and now they're all trying to persuade her and no one's taking it seriously, least of all her. And I have to pretend I think it's a joke, too.'

Anne and Dr Barry were arguing. He was holding her lightly by the elbow and making as if to go with her. She was shaking her head. Not wanting to be left standing alone, Robert went with Tim to the drinks table beneath the tree.

Tim ladled out the Pimms. 'Point is, this is the last night it's possible before her Schools.'

'Dinner?'

'Anything.'

67

Dr Barry rejoined the girls on the lawn. Anne had disappeared. Tim put the Pimms in Robert's hand. 'One more try. See you later.'

Robert watched him rejoin Suzanne and the two other girls. There was a burst of laughter at something he said. Robert's Pimms disappeared with puzzling rapidity. He poured himself another, feeling unnaturally clear-headed: a bad sign.

'Why did you cancel tonight's rehearsal?' Gina stood before him. Her voice was more abrupt than usual.

'We overdid it yesterday. They were so tired they weren't remembering anything. And as most were going to be here tonight they wouldn't have been much good afterwards.'

'I didn't know it was cancelled until I met Stephen on the way here.'

'Jackie was supposed to have told you.' Her accusatory tone caused him to suppress any note of apology.

'Well, she didn't. We should have rehearsed tonight. We're nowhere near good enough.'

'I know, but I decided to give it a rest.'

'I thought you were supposed to be a perfectionist.'

'I didn't know that.'

They stared at each other. He had the impression she was on the verge of smiling.

'Why did you choose Malcolm?'

'He was a good Mirabel and I gave him the benefit of the doubt at the audition.'

'That was a mistake.'

'I know.'

'He hasn't got it. No timing, no dramatic sense. I don't think it's going to be a very good production.'

It was true but he wasn't ready to admit it. 'You will have to make up for him. Carry him.'

She shrugged and continued to stare. Again he thought she almost smiled. He wondered if she were drunk. She held out her glass. 'Will you get me another drink?'

He poured himself one as well, feeling exhilarated but

bereft of inspiration. 'What will you do when you leave Oxford?'

She looked amused and scornful. 'Are you trying to chat me up?'

'I wondered. I was interested. It'll pass.'

'I haven't thought about what I'll do.'

'Go into the theatre.'

'I'm not that dedicated. Anyway, I've got another year, don't forget.' She drank and pushed back her hair. 'I hope you're not waiting to be asked the same boring question.'

'You'd get the same boring answer.'

'That pregnant girl you were talking to — is she the one married to Dr Barry?'

'Yes.'

'She must be miserable.'

'Why?'

'Well, look at him. And you used to go out with her, didn't you?'

'Yes.'

She was smiling now. 'I don't believe in marriage. They're all so wretched. I suppose you do.'

'I've never thought about it.'

'I don't believe that, either.' She continued smiling. 'Can you imagine yourself loving anyone?'

He shrugged but overdid it and nearly spilled his drink. 'Why not? As much as I can imagine anyone else, whatever it means.'

'I can imagine you being horribly passionate and intense but not loving.'

'You're not usually so full of compliments.'

'I think I'm being restrained. Do you love anyone at the moment?'

'Well, it depends what you — '

She laughed suddenly. 'You do, don't you? You're about to say you're in love. Which you're not really, of course.'

'No, I'm not.' His denial was more forceful than he'd intended.

'Not what?' She laughed again. 'Come on — not in love or not about to say it?'

He turned away, grinning, and picked up the jug to replenish their glasses. 'Are you as drunk as I am?'

'Probably.' She stood very close. He kept noticing a small blue vein in her neck. 'Why don't you take me out to dinner?' she asked.

'I'm going to see someone.'

She raised her eyebrows, turned and walked away. He lifted his brimful glass to his lips whilst watching her but spilled it down his chin and on to his T-shirt. He was still dabbing clumsily at it with his handkerchief when Tim approached him again.

'Done it,' said Tim.

'Well done.'

'It'll cost a packet. Not that that matters.'

'Where are you taking her?'

'Them. All three of them. To the Elizabeth because they know it's the most expensive. Not sure that's true, but never mind. She wouldn't come alone.'

'Have a nice time.'

'The difficulty will be finding a reason for going back to her place afterwards.' Tim looked from Robert to Dr Barry and back. His tone softened. 'Come with us, unless you've got plans for tonight.'

'Thanks, but I'm going to go and see someone.'

Tim nodded. 'Good luck.'

Robert remained beneath the tree. It was dusk now and the lighter-coloured shirts and dresses looked disembodied in the gloom. The sky was still fragile and clear and a few small stars were already showing through. The Mozart had stopped.

Michael Mann was sitting on the grass with a dozen or so people who were all laughing at someone mimicking. Dr Barry and his group of girls moved over to join them. He glanced at Robert but gave no sign of recognition. Robert stepped back behind the trestle tables and walked round two sides of the cloisters, passing slowly from pillar to pillar. On the walls were memorial tablets to men of the college and a long list of the Great War dead. Three or four were disconcertingly recent, victims of accidents, drownings or diseases picked up whilst travelling during the vacs. He still had his Pimms in his hand when he reached the archway. He looked at it, drank it all, then very deliberately placed the empty glass on the low stone wall.

Robert knocked again. There was a light on in the kitchen but that was all. The absence of bikes in the garden meant that the lodgers must also be out. He waited a while at the top of the steps, leaning against the wall. It had not occurred to him that she might not be back. Whenever he was determined on something and prevented by some accidental but crucial factor he persisted with a dogged obstinacy well beyond the point of hopelessness, convinced the state of affairs was so unfair it had to come right. It felt unfair because he had been frustrated by chance, not because he had been defeated in battle or found wanting when the time came to trial. As he waited now, though, he was rewarded; he remembered Anne saying once that Yale Gail had mislaid her keys so frequently that Dr Barry had hidden a spare set beneath the laurel so that she could let herself in. He went on hands and knees into the laurels, feeling carefully because he could see very little, and quickly found the half brick with the keys underneath. He unlocked the door, replaced the keys and went in.

It was a big house, rambling, untidy, quiet, the sort of place he thought he might like for himself one day. He could imagine Tim living in it and filling it with antiques and damask. There were signs of a hastily finished meal in the kitchen. The only sounds were an occasional grumble from the Rayburn and the ticking of a red alarm clock on the kitchen shelf. He sat in an old Windsor chair by the window.

Robert did not have Tim's gift for waiting. Tim could

wait as cattle wait, in a ruminative trance, passively, without expectation. For Robert, waiting was a form of activity that had to be pursued like other forms, with determination.

When eventually he heard a key in the door it struck him that she might not be alone. He sat stiffly until he heard her slow footfall in the hall. She entered the kitchen and stopped, her handbag held loosely in both hands and her hat still down over her eyes. Her belly looked bigger than ever.

'I didn't mean to surprise you,' he said, unembarrassed by his dishonesty.

'You haven't.'

She walked over to the window and pulled the curtains behind his head. 'Do you want a drink, or tea?'

'Tea.'

She put on a kettle, emptied the teapot in the sink and washed a couple of blue-and-white striped mugs. Next she went out into the hall and returned without her hat and wearing slippers. Her hair was tied back in a bun, making her face look fuller and more purposeful. He remembered that that was how she had her hair when he first saw her, working, in Duke Humfrey's Room in the Old Bodleian. After three days of discreet but unsuccessful observation he had had to resort to looking over her shoulder at her reader's ticket while pretending to consult Gauden's *Ecclesia Suspiria* in the shelf behind.

'David staying on at the party?' he asked, to see if she knew when he'd be back.

'Looks like it.'

'Are you unhappy?'

She looked calmly at him. 'No, I'm very happy. We both are.'

'Why did you say what you did about the baby?'

She shrugged and half smiled. 'I was being silly. Probably my condition.' She spoke the words as if they were in inverted commas. 'I feel needlessly overwrought sometimes.'

72

It would have been easy to go on and be normal but he felt a cold determination, of which wanting to get at the truth was only a part.

'Is it David's baby, then?'

'Of course it is.'

She poured from the electric kettle and put the cups and the milk on the table. She sat while the tea brewed. He tried to work out whether the baby could in fact have been his, and concluded it could, just, at least insofar as he understood the theory of such things. However, he felt better now that he had asked and wanted to be conciliatory.

She sat side on to the table, her head resting in her hand and her face mostly hidden from him. With her other hand she picked at a splinter of the table's edge. He tried to remember making love with her. She was such a different shape now that looking didn't help. The more explicitly he tried to recall the less clearly he could remember.

'The party wasn't bad, was it?' he said and then, feeling she would not reply, continued quickly. 'It was a relief to leave, though. Always is.'

She said something but her voice was so muffled he had to ask her to repeat it. She put both her hands to her face and her shoulders shook.

Tears reduced Robert to tenderness and guilt. He stood by her chair and put his hands on her shoulders. When he spoke her name she got up and turned in one swift movement, pressing her face against him.

Her grip loosened and she stood back. She rubbed something off his neck with her hand, her eyes downcast. 'I'm so tired I can't explain. You never listen to what I say, you always try to make me say things in a way I don't really mean. And you're so cold and distant, I don't know what you want. I don't think you want anything, not really, you just go on wanting. It's always you, it's never me.' She put her hand to her face again.

He pulled her gently to him, mistaking passivity for

acquiescence, feeling at once a surge of tenderness and a small secret thrill of triumph. Keeping his stomach drawn in, so as not to press too much against hers, he bent to kiss her. Despite her bulk, she twisted like a cat in his arms. He glimpsed her face and her raised arm. He had in fact time to avoid the blow but did not. It was harder than he was prepared for, hot and stinging, knocking his head sideways. For a moment they stared at each other. Her face was flushed and her brown eyes hot and excited. One side of his jaw ached.

She raised her hand again but he caught it, then grabbed the other. She pulled and pushed, her head bent, trying to kick him. He kept saying her name but she kept pushing and pulling in a silent ineffectual frenzy. He had visions of her miscarrying, of Dr Barry walking in, of her collapsing and dying. His thigh knocked the table hard and something fell, her head hit his lip painfully. Her breath came in gasps.

Quite suddenly she stopped struggling, went limp and swayed towards him. He put his arms round her, trying both to hold gently and support her but she folded at the knees. He knew he would be unable to hold without squeezing and so he fell with her, slowly, one hand clutching the bar in front of the Rayburn. He managed to keep her on top and a little to his side. Her head was against his face, her hair in his mouth.

He asked a couple of times if she was all right but got no answer.

For a few moments he felt he was sliding into panic but he stopped himself by an act of will. It was remarkably easy. He had only to say no and he became immediately fatalistic; it was serious and absurd, it mattered and it didn't.

He was relieved, though, when she shifted to a more comfortable position. Her voluminous dress had risen up her thighs and one leg which now seemed incongruously thin lay across his. Still without speaking, she slowly moved her face from his shoulder and bit his arm. At first he lay still. The pain was sharp but he could make himself isolate it, consider it a thing apart as when he was running. When it deepened viciously he tried to pull his arm away but the top half of her body was upon it. He turned suddenly on his side, knocking the table leg and making something fall, then bit where her shoulder met her neck. Her dress tasted of washing powder and scent. The worse the pain in his arm the harder he bit. He had started to bite very hard, clenching his jaw, when she let go with a gasp. He did the same and felt her whole body soften. He kept his lips on the spot he had bitten.

After a while she slowly raised herself to a sitting position, leaning against the table leg. She eased her legs carefully to the side, one hand on her stomach. He sat with his arm round her shoulders.

'Are you sure you're all right?' he asked.

She nodded. She seemed in no hurry to get up. He was torn between persuading her, at the risk of moving when perhaps she shouldn't, and remaining on the floor at the risk of being found there by Dr Barry. They could say she had fallen. He already felt shabby for thinking it.

'I don't know,' she said quietly. 'The answer to your question, I mean.'

He felt no excitement but rather the opposite, a kind of deadening within. 'You don't know whether it's his or mine?'

'No.'

For a while his mind was occupied trying to work out the timings, how quickly she must have begun with Dr Barry.

'Will you help me up?'

He helped her to her feet. She smoothed down her dress, pushed back some of her hair that had come loose and picked up a mug that had fallen over on the table. Her face was heavy now, puffed and blotched. 'It might be better if you went,' she said.

He did not move. 'And the other question?'

Her brown eyes were impenetrably full. 'Oh, yes, I am happy. I'm very happy. We both are.'

It was later than he realized. He walked fast, away from Norham Gardens and away from the centre. The city was quiet. He wanted not to notice where he was going but it was necessary always to decide. He walked up the Banbury Road to Summertown, across to the Woodstock Road and back down but he still wanted to avoid going back to college.

He headed instead towards Jericho, an area of narrow streets formed by small nineteenth-century houses, once a red-light district but now middle-class and fashionable. Young couples, newly married or self-consciously unmarried, bought their first homes and put in heating. Some of the unmodernized houses were still let to students. He decided he would walk through Jericho, over the canal and railway and on to Portmeadow where he could wander in the dark without being able to see more than the Isis or the horizon. Entering one street, though, he recognized the house where Gina lived. He had visited it when telling her she had the part. It was the fourth down and she shared it with a fluctuating number of students.

Her bedroom was the former sitting room, to the right of the front door. A dim light showed through the curtains. He knocked on the window pane. The edge of the curtain twitched and he stood back so that she could see him under the street lamp. The door opened a few seconds later.

Her hair was tousled as if she had been lying down. He walked in without speaking and stood in her room while she closed the doors. He had no idea what he was going to do.

Her smile was indulgent but slightly mocking. 'Was your lady not in?'

He sat. 'I'd like a drink.'

There was an opened bottle of red wine on the floor by her desk.

'There's only this plonk.'

He nodded. The room was small and untidy. A radio-cassette played soul music quietly in the corner. On the narrow bed was a volume of Sylvia Plath's poetry. Around the walls were posters of plays Gina had been in. She handed him the wine. 'You don't look happy.'

It tasted hard and bitter. He drank quickly, then reached for the bottle and drank from that. She sat cross-legged on the bed, her back against the wall and her face framed by her tousled hair. She wore yellow jeans and balanced her wine carefully on her foot in front of her crotch.

'I want you to do something for me.' He suspected he might be slurring his words.

'What?'

'Take off your clothes.'

She gazed unsmilingly at him with a gentle almost maternal expression, then got slowly off the bed and put her glass on the desk. She pulled her shirt over her head, shaking her hair free, and eased off each plimsoll with the other foot as she unzipped her jeans. She took off her white knickers and tossed them aside. Her triangle of hair was dark and tightly curled, her thighs slightly plump. She stared at him with the same calm expression.

The music had stopped and he felt hot. The room seemed to be smaller, pressing in on him. Some people walked past the window, talking and laughing, alarmingly close and loud. He lowered the bottle to the floor by his chair and stood. She continued to stare.

He walked past and out, out of the house, leaving both doors open. He walked quickly and unsteadily, still towards Portmeadow but noticing no more.

Chapter Five

Failure was always more tiring than success and when Tim returned to college late that evening he felt heavy-limbed and hopeless. The Elizabeth had been full so he had taken the three girls to La Sorbonne, which was as good and probably no less expensive. They had had a good time, as had he so long as he had the prospect of progress before him, but when he walked them back to St Hilda's Suzanne made good use of the presence of her friends. She was effusive in her thanks, affectionate in her farewells, permitting him no chance of seeing her alone. In fact, her last words had been that she would see him after Schools.

Approaching college reminded him of work. Another day with no progress on that front either, though as the time of reckoning approached he found he cared less. He would get a degree, he supposed. As for afterwards, there was nothing he wanted, just as there was nothing he lacked.

Chetwynd stood at the bottom of Tim's staircase, embracing four or five bottles of wine, a moist light in his eyes.

'Take me to your room. I must not stop drinking and will not drink alone.'

Tim did not want company and the prospect of Chetwynd was exhausting. But it didn't matter; nothing did.

Chetwynd spoke with gentle deliberation. 'I am annihilated. Drinking since I saw you. First with Orpwood then with others unknown. Your arm, please.'

They climbed the stairs carefully. 'Nice of you to bring the odd bottle.'

'I shall drink more than I bring. I stole them.'

'Who from?'

'Someone's party. Don't ask whose. I was thrown out of a car on the Cowley Road outside a house with loud music and people. So I walked in, more or less straight, accused a meek-looking girl of drinking my wine and sent her off to get me another. The bottles were near an open window so I sat there and quietly put a few on the sill outside. I had some more wine, borrowed some matches – just to be sociable – went to the garden for a pee and left with the bottles. How many more steps are there?'

'We're on the landing now.'

'I am royally drunk.'

'I think you are.'

'It destroys balance, vision, coordination but not speech, which is odd. If I have the good fortune to die when drunk I shall probably continue talking until rigor mortis sets in. No one will notice till then.'

He sat on the floor of Tim's room with the bottles lined up beside him and laboriously filled his pipe. 'Before I leave tonight I have something to ask of you. Remind me. Now to drink. You choose.'

Tim looked at the assortment of cheap wine. He was not, after all, indifferent to everything. 'I've got some better stuff than that.'

'It would be wasted.'

'It's a waste if it's not drunk. Or we could go straight on to the malt.'

Chetwynd took his pipe from his mouth. 'Now I hear you.'

'Do you want some matches? I'm not sure I have any.'

'I have some.'

'Aren't you going to light it, then?'

'I have.'

'You think so?'

Chetwynd looked at his pipe. 'You shouldn't have told me. I thought I was enjoying that smoke.'

Much later Robert joined them. He had rambled for over two hours in Portmeadow, and his shoes, socks and jeans were soaked by the dew. His jeans were also muddied down one side where he had stumbled over a cow that was lying down. It had heaved beneath him like an earthquake and left him sprawling.

Chetwynd was by then stretched out on the floor with his eyes closed. Tim lay in one of the armchairs, a bowl of cereal mixed with whisky in his lap. He grinned and made a wide welcoming gesture with his spoon.

'Who is it?' asked Chetwynd. He held up one hand for Robert to shake. 'I would embrace you but getting up would be tedious and undignified. Forgive my closed eyes. We were discussing despair.'

'Why?'

'Why, indeed. Because your friend here still nurses a secret desire to find some point in life. He denies it but I know him better than he knows himself. He'll never find one. He knows that, too, in his soul. He's doomed.'

Tim grinned and tried to speak through a mouthful of cornflakes but coughed. When Chetwynd heard the clink of the whisky bottle on Robert's glass he raised his own to be filled. He could not hold it still and some of the whisky spilled on to his face, causing his tongue to become active around his lips.

Robert sat on the floor by the door.

'Find her?' asked Tim sleepily. Robert nodded. 'Lot of mud on your jeans. She throw you out of the window?'

'That was Portmeadow. Nice dinner?'

'Nice social dinner. Gratifyingly expensive. All for nothing.'

Chetwynd opened his eyes. 'Did I ever tell you I can't get an erection with a woman unless I know her well? Sometimes I have to know her for months. Do you not think that strange?'

'Sensitive,' said Tim.

'But when I'm not with her I get an erection every time I think of her.'

'Scared of women,' said Robert.

'Most men are but it doesn't affect them like that.'

'You have a chronic disease of the soul. Nothing is real for you unless you have imagined it.'

Chetwynd laughed silently. 'Go on.'

'You can't accept any experience directly. You have to detach it from its original and recast it as you want it.'

'More, more.'

'You are frightened of everything.'

'Is that all?'

'It's enough.'

The empty bowl slid from Tim's knees to the floor and rolled under the table. 'End of the cornflakes,' he said.

Chetwynd held up both arms. 'Would you mind helping me up?' They tried but it was not easy. He started to laugh and twice they all ended up on the floor. Eventually they propped him against the wall between the window and the bookcase.

He stood for some time with his eyes closed and did not speak until he opened them. 'Before I go,' he said, then paused as if mentally rehearsing each step of a long and hazardous journey. 'Before I go there is a favour. I mentioned it a hundred years ago on the stairs. Will you do it for me, both of you?'

'What?' asked Tim.

'Agree first. Friendship demands.'

'Doesn't demand that much.'

'The essence of a favour is being predisposed to commit yourself to it. Is that pompous enough for you?'

'Okay.'

Robert nodded. Chetwynd took his glass from the table where Tim had put it and swallowed more whisky. His Adam's apple bobbed twice. 'I have a gun,' he said quietly. 'I tell you before showing you so that you know I'm not about to shoot us all in a fit of Schools' madness.'

After some fumbling he pulled from the pocket of his

81

corduroys a small heavy-looking revolver with a short barrel. 'Don't ask me how I got it. There's also a bullet.' He displayed the bullet in the palm of his hand. 'The favour is, I want you to keep both for me in case during a fit of euphoria I shoot myself before leaving this place. I'll have them back after Schools.'

Neither spoke. For the first time the ticking of the clock in Tim's bedroom made itself noticeable.

'I loathe examinations,' Chetwynd concluded. 'One or two people kill themselves every year over Schools, so why not me? Of course, I'd do it publicly, make a drama of it, splattering my brains across the front desk after handing my papers to the invigilator. I imagine him picking bits of membrane from his gown.' He mimed a fastidious and urbane invigilator. 'You're right, Robert, I have to imagine it first. That's because I don't really want to do it, you see. Not yet, anyway. But the temptation remains. When I'm drunk I sometimes amuse myself with Russian roulette.' He grinned. 'Isn't that a cliché?'

They smiled back.

'You don't know whether to take me seriously. I know the feeling. Watch.' He broke the gun, slotted the bullet into the chamber and spun it a couple of times. Then he put the barrel to his head just in front of one ear and, grinning again and with his eyes open, squeezed the trigger.

There was a dull click. Everything was as before.

Chetwynd unloaded his gun. 'Still here, you see. I had to make you believe. Wouldn't expect you to take my word alone.' He rested the gun on the table and stood the bullet on its base beside it. 'And I do it for ever more trivial reasons, that's the danger. It's masturbatory, of course, ever my joy and solace. But I don't want to die here. I want to die in London. Don't ask me why, I hate the place. So, will you do it? Keep them from me until I ask for them back?'

The clock was audible again. Robert recalled his conversation with Hansford about guns. It had seemed absurd

82

then but now seemed safe. He felt wearily sober. 'Why not just give us the bullet? Comes to the same thing.'

'No, it must be both. It's more difficult then for me to break in and get them.'

Robert sipped his whisky without enthusiasm, feeling Tim's glance upon him. He held out his hand. Chetwynd tossed the bullet and he caught it. He put it on the floor and rolled it backwards and forwards with his fingers.

Chetwynd pushed the revolver across the table to Tim, then pulled back one of the velvet curtains. The sun was just up and the brickwork of the New Building was offensively bright. Far beyond, the light touched the trees of Wytham Wood, making everything in the room seem tawdry and unreal.

Tim rubbed his pale face. 'That's blown it. Another day, another night.'

Chetwynd held on to the curtain. 'Thank you both. We live through sympathy and through nothing else. We are dead otherwise. My father was a vicar.' He sounded as if he meant to go on but stopped and remained without looking up. 'He died. Yours haven't yet, I suppose?'

'Mine left,' said Tim. 'When I was twelve. Two stepfathers.'

Chetwynd nodded. 'A full bladder makes me want to talk piss as well as do it. May I?'

'Be my guest.'

He pushed the revolver farther aside, knelt on the table and opened the bottom half of the window. 'Who lives below?'

'Hansford.'

'He'll think it's early morning rain on his windowsill. Dawn is so depressing.'

'He may have clothes hanging out to dry,' said Robert.

Chetwynd was framed against the daylight. He raised both hands and shook with silent laughter.

The Middle Eastern situation worsened. The American fleet was reinforced and there was talk of a blockade.

When an American aircraft carrier and its shadowing Russian minesweeper collided, with no damage to either, there was excited television and press comment to the effect that this was the sort of incident that could begin a third world war. The Royal Navy committed a ship to the area.

There was frequent speculation about the reintroduction of conscription and about the immediate use of chemical weapons by the Soviet army in what one newspaper called 'the introductory pre-nuclear exchange'. There were rumours, started and repeated solely by the press, about the making and issuing of sixty million chemical protection suits (CPSs) and respirators. Married middle-class women in their thirties flocked to join peace groups and some enterprising firms did a brisk trade in fall-out shelters. The Government did nothing.

Fortunately the crisis was not so dire as to interfere with Eights Week, the inter-college rowing championship. This took place in the fifth week of term and was the climax of the rowing year. The city — at least the university part of it that someone had aptly dubbed 'the Latin Quarter of Cowley' — took on a carnival atmosphere. The sun burned unabated, lectures were deserted, revisions neglected, tutorials postponed. Christ Church meadows thronged with undergraduates drinking in the college boathouses. Some went up river to shout at the eights, others lay supine in the grass.

The college had a good chance of becoming Head of the River and so was practically empty. Even Orpwood, who disdained sport and used the absence of opposition to plaster the Junior Common Room with Stop the War posters, was twice seen on the river, a can of beer in his hand.

Tim went in the afternoon following the night with Chetwynd. He had set out to work and had got as far as the library. Guilt left him now that he was strolling contentedly among the crowds. It was a relief to be in company and see no one he knew, to be ungreeted and unknown, until he ran into Hansford.

Hansford pressed a beer on him and talked for twenty minutes about the rowing. He had done a wholehearted job in the college third eight which had been bumped — defeated — the day before. It was all the fault of the cox, apparently.

Tim felt he had to do something to show gratitude for his beer. 'Talking of bumping, has anyone had a go at you yet?'

Hansford lowered his can and looked from side to side. 'Not yet, but I'm not dropping my guard. This Iraqi geezer's still coming, remember. They might try and coincide it with that. The worse the crisis gets the more the Lefties will try to stir up trouble at home.'

'I suppose so.'

'Things are pretty bad.' Hansford looked solemn. 'In fact, I'm wondering whether I shouldn't give up accountancy and try for a commission. Trouble is, if there is a war it might be over by the time I'd finished training.'

'So might the world.'

'That too.'

Tim did not see Robert until the following morning when he was trying out a new blend of coffee.

Robert was vigorous and cheerful. 'I could smell it from the quad.'

They normally saw each other daily but Robert seemed unaware of the lapse. 'I made some yesterday, too,' said Tim.

'Yesterday.' Robert made it sound a very long time ago. 'Yesterday — I went back to Portmeadow and slept. A pint and a half in the Perch, then rehearsals.'

'No work?'

'No work.'

'I may forgive you.'

'I hope so. I have a favour.'

'Not another gun?'

85

'No. What have you done with it?'

Tim tapped the table. 'In the drawer. Don't know where else to put it. Under the mattress seemed so corny. Where's the bullet?'

Robert forced his hand into the pocket of jeans and produced the bullet after a struggle. 'It's so difficult to get out I can't lose it.'

'Do you think he was serious?'

'The Russian roulette bit was pretty convincing.'

'He's gone to ground now. Not even a light in his room.' He waited, making Robert wait. 'Well?'

Robert grinned. 'A lift to Minster Lovell. There's an old Jaguar.'

Tim slapped his thigh and laughed. Whenever he laughed it sounded false, Robert reflected. Smiling suited Tim better.

'I'll take you to Minster Lovell on condition we include the Old Swan.'

From the security of owning a BMW Tim followed with relish each of Robert's automotive adventures. Robert had had many cars, all from the bottom end of the market, and they were the major cause of his financial ruin. Two terms before he had nearly been sent down for non-payment of college bills and battels but had been bailed out by Tim. He had then had to work on a building site throughout the vac and had sold his coat and some of his books in order to repay him, though Tim neither wanted nor needed the money. It was the closest they had come to serious disagreement. Tim was still pleased to be asked any favour.

'Jesus, it must be getting bad,' he said. 'What are you trying to buy your way out of now — Schools, the play, Anne and Dr Barry and all that?'

'Come on, I've been restrained all this term. It's been building up.'

'Only because your last little affair bankrupted you. What is this Jag?'

'Fifteen years old. Very cheap. Still has an MOT. They're bound to appreciate one day.'

'You were still saying that about the Armstrong the day they came to take it away. You're off your head. Everyone has trouble with old Jags. Oil, rust, petrol. And two days ago you wanted that Daimler Majestic. Anyway, what are you going to buy it with?'

'I'm in credit with the insurance on the Armstrong. I'm getting the money back and I'll use part of it to insure the Jag for a month and the rest to buy it. It's taxed for a month, too. Also, I wouldn't use it much, hardly at all, so it wouldn't cost much in petrol. In fact, it could be regarded as a financial discipline, a way of saving.'

'Go on.'

'I've never had an old Jaguar.'

'Don't.'

'It's red.'

'Buy a mini and paint it.'

Robert raised his arms in a gesture of hopelessness, as of one in the thrall of vast impersonal forces. His desire for cars had never had anything to do with need.

'An old Jag', continued Tim, 'with its ends knocked out and its pistons coming through the crankcase, is not a car, it's a concept. You are seeking a concept of yourself — an even more self-destructive one than usual. You must be changing.'

'Maybe I'm finding the right one at last.'

'Again.'

They set off in the BMW with the sun roof open and at Tim's usual exhilarating pace. He loaded the cassette player and spent most of the journey adjusting it to his meticulous ear. Robert rested his arm on the door and gazed contentedly down the valley of the Windrush.

'Do you think Chetwynd would really do it?' Tim had to raise his voice above the wind and music.

'He almost did, didn't he?'

'Not that I'm blaming him. I mean, why not, when you come to look at it? What's so special?'

87

'It's a nice day, that's why not. You may as well go on as long as you enjoy it.'

'That all?'

Robert raised his hands.

The Jaguar did not live up to its advertisement. 'Mechanically sound' included oil pressure that dropped significantly after high revving and 'good for year' bodywork that was bad even for that. There had been a rough respray on the front wings and the interior was scruffy. The seller, a young man with a wispy moustache and dull downcast eyes, said he was unemployed, had worked in a garage and was now setting himself up in the motor trade. He lived in a council house with three sallow children and an unhappy-looking wife. Robert bought the car.

Tim hovered while the haggling went on, embarrassed. The agreed price was appropriately low. Robert had to leave what he had on him as a deposit. The man was to deliver the car to Oxford when Robert had the rest of the money.

'You're out of your skull,' Tim said as they drove away.

'I liked the feel of it.'

'You won't when you start feeling with your pocket.'

'But I feel better.'

'And it's a nice day, don't tell me.'

The Old Swan was on the bank of the Windrush in the quaint part of the village. The restaurant was closed, to Tim's intense disappointment, and they had to sit by an empty fireplace with chicken and chips. Tim picked at his before offering the remains to Robert who scooped it on to his plate.

'Does anything affect your appetite?' Tim asked.

'Food and the lack of it. You?'

Tim sighed. 'The way they're fried.'

When they left Tim offered Robert the chance to drive. He was normally very protective of his car but the sun, the beer, the reassuring sound of a distant lawnmower and a general carelessness, a wish to be rid of things, all combined. After an inconclusive discussion about insurance they meandered back through the lanes. On one bend they had a clear view of the ravages of Dutch Elm disease, field after field lined with dead trees.

'Looks like the war's already happened,' said Tim.

They were nearing Swinbrook when a pale ginger cat jumped from the cow parsley on the nearside bank. Robert braked hard and stopped. 'I didn't feel anything, did you?'

Tim looked back. 'Can't see it.'

'I thought I heard a thump, though.'

'Maybe.'

They saw nothing when they first got out. The afternoon was hot and silent. It seemed likely that the cat had escaped into the field on the other side of the lane. It was Tim who heard the faint hissing. The cat was on its back, beneath the rear axle.

Robert pulled the car forward so that the creature was exposed. It lay on the tarmac, writhing with the top half of its body only. Its mouth was open and it hissed with every breath. A car came the other way, slowed and passed on.

'It can't live,' said Tim.

'Could take hours to die.'

'Better kill it.'

'Put it out of its agony.'

They spoke to reassure each other. Robert climbed the bank and found a large stone and a stick.

'You going to do it?'

'I was driving.' Robert considered his weapons. Smashing its head with the stone would be the surest, breaking its skull like an eggshell. But that seemed gratuitously brutal, as if deliberately overdoing it. He could run it over again but that was cumbersome. He decided to break its neck with a single blow from the stick.

He raised the stick with both hands and brought it down hard across the cat's throat. The body jumped and the stick broke on the road, leaving him holding only a foot or so of wood. The cat jerked and twitched in slow spasms, its hissing weak and irregular.

'I'll get another one,' Robert said with forced calm, and climbed up the bank again. Tim said something he didn't catch. He turned in time to see him raise the stone with both hands and bring it down on the animal's head. The hissing stopped.

A blackbird sang, close by, and above them, louder, nearer and nearer, a jet made its approach to Brize Norton. Tim edged the stone aside with his foot. The cat's head was intact but thinner and there was blood in its lips.

Robert dragged it by one warm hind leg to the side of the road. 'Thanks.' Tim said nothing. 'Where do you think it comes from?'

'Dunno.'

Tim seemed listless, indifferent, more than calm. Robert had to make an effort to control his voice. 'Not much point in asking.'

'No.'

He offered the keys but Tim shook his head. 'You carry on.'

Robert did not want to drive but told himself it was absurd to be so upset over a cat. Upset over nothing because it was nothing now. There had been something to be upset about before but now there was nothing at all. 'Thanks.' he said again, briskly.

Neither spoke until they were on the main road.

'Maybe not such a nice day,' said Robert.

Tim shrugged. 'Not nice for us, okay for the cat.'

'Not very okay.'

'Put the feeling aside. There's nothing else then.'

Robert drove cautiously at first but found it was making him brood. He felt better going faster. He overtook two lorries and had to swerve to avoid an oncoming third.

'Sight of blood whet your appetite?' murmured Tim, without looking round.

*

90

Dr Barry was restless and sharp in tutorials, often amusing, sometimes petulant. He would cross and uncross his legs and scratch his head or ankle vigorously when making a point. When bored or impatient he would end the tutorial abruptly. Tim avoided revision tutorials but Robert attended one because he had chosen an ethics and philosophy of religion option that was open to theologians. Like the lecture, it was a way of avoiding serious work.

He arrived late for the revision class that afternoon. The sherry had already been round, Dr Barry was in high good humour and he sprawled in his armchair with one leg over the side and scratched his shin with a ruler. 'Glass in the cupboard, Robert. Help yourself.'

There were eight or nine others, some sitting on the floor. Robert had to squat against Dr Barry's chair and face them. He hoped he would not have to contribute. It was soon clear that Dr Barry was not confining himself to the Schools paper but was trotting out some of his hobby-horses.

'Same with ethics,' he said, with a wave of his ruler. 'Disguised moralizing. All this agonizing from people like Hare. Ridiculous. Wretched stuff.'

He moved from ethics to philosophy of religion, on which there were likely to be only a couple of questions. Two too many, he thought. He was cheerfully atheistic and tried to provoke his class but they responded reluctantly. What little intellectual curiosity they possessed quickly evaporated in the face of Schools. They wanted to be told what to write in their papers.

'You're a lot of dumplings this afternoon. Robert.' He rested the ruler on Robert's head. 'Would you say that the end of all religion is consolation?'

Robert, recalled from a trance-like vacancy, said what first came into his head. 'I think it would be the end.'

Dr Barry laughed and his bare lower leg jerked up and down. 'Just as all true romances end in marriage. Where's the sherry? I'd give you something stronger only the tutor's allowance won't run to it.'

The discussion moved on to utilitarianism and became a brisk canter. Robert drifted back into his near-cataleptic state. The talk became background and he felt very drowsy. He was vividly and intermittently aware of detail. The rough texture of the armchair, the light catching someone's pale sherry, a shout in the quad, a remark about rule utilitarianism, all struck with temporarily unbalancing force but were insufficient to recall him. There followed a kind of inner fall, a deep and piercing sadness. It was the realization that everything important had been got wrong, that it could all still be got right if only it could be seen differently, that none of it ever would be. If only the sadness, the sadness everyone carried around in him, were visible to all, all might yet be well. It was very close, just below the surface, but it would never happen. Buchner's stars, he remembered, were God's tears. God was weeping for us.

The discussion ended. Robert got unsteadily to his feet as if moving too soon after a deep sleep. The others were mutedly going through the formalities of leave-taking. Dr Barry remarked cheerfully that it was the last time he would see them before Schools and they left his room as if for the gallows.

He put his hand on Robert's arm. 'Hang on, I want a word.'

It was the last thing that Robert wanted and Dr Barry was the last person he wanted it with. He felt immediately guilty.

'I've got to go, I've got something arranged — a rehearsal.'

'What time?'

He hesitated too long under Dr Barry's eager ferret-like gaze. 'Well, I've — that's what I've got to arrange.'

'Come and have tea. At home, not here. Anne wanted me to ask you.'

'I'm not sure — '

'She'll blame me if you don't come. She was most insistent. I think as her time draws near' — he smiled quickly — 'she likes to have her old friends around her, as it were.' He smiled again.

The walk up to Norham Gardens was a long way to fill with conversation. Robert prepared himself to gush about the play, to talk about his other papers in theology, even to discuss ethics. Nothing that Dr Barry usually said was directly threatening but Robert had the uneasy feeling that he himself was well understood. In the event there was hardly any need to say anything. Dr Barry talked about his first wife.

'Barefoot and pregnant, that's when she was happiest. They usually are. The pain, the discomfort, they put up with it all. Much more than we would, you know.' He glanced at Robert. 'It's almost nothing to do with us, really. Of course, there's emotional dependence but that varies. As for the rest — blood — blood means nothing. How can it? A man can't tell his newborn baby from any other, provided they're all the same colour.'

They were passing Keble, which had scaffolding outside festooned with Stop the War posters. Robert made use of it to avoid having to look at Dr Barry.

'Do you still see your other children?'

'See them, feed them, clothe them, house them. Some things never change.' Dr Barry laughed sourly. 'No, but for the woman it's the first one that really makes the difference. It's not the pregnancy or the birth, it's having a completely dependent baby around for twenty-four hours a day. They don't know what's hit them. I keep trying to prepare Anne but you can't, really. Whatever I say doesn't mean anything yet. That's why I hope you won't stop coming to see her after the birth. They need to learn that the rest of the world goes on. Helps restore perspective.'

Robert nodded, keeping his gaze on the pavement.

Anne was again in the high-ceilinged kitchen, this time washing a great many cups and mugs and stacking them

93

in the drying rack. She embraced Robert and kissed him on the lips without having glanced at Dr Barry, who went immediately to the bread bin. Robert was awkward in the embrace, trying not to press against her.

She smiled. 'No need to be afraid, I won't explode.'

They had toast and tea and what Robert supposed would be called a general discussion. This was the sort he always found most difficult. Dr Barry read the paper and seemed to pay little attention. Robert's conversation with Anne felt like a very rapid game of table tennis.

She had been to the pre-natal clinic. 'I'm really looking forward to it now. The birth, I mean. Before I just wanted to get it over with but now I actually want it to happen.'

She had said the same thing twice very recently and he just stopped himself from asking if the baby was still due when it was due. Instead, he asked what she was going to do after the baby was born. Asking questions was an easy way of seeming to talk.

'It depends.' She dipped a custard cream into her tea, waiting for the drips to fall before moving it to her lips. 'Obviously, I'll finish my doctorate but what then is the problem. Academic jobs aren't exactly easy to come by, especially here. I've wondered about doing something quite different, like qualifying as a solicitor. I know it takes a long time but you can practise more or less anywhere and you can do it part-time.'

'Make a lot of money, too,' said Dr Barry, without looking up from his paper.

'What about you?' she asked Robert. 'You used to say you were going into the Church. Are you still?'

Robert let his eyes wander the wide, tangled garden. The idea of himself taking holy orders had become unfamiliar, like stories told by his parents about incidents in his childhood which he could not remember. 'Did I say that? Actually say it?'

She smiled. 'If you didn't you did a pretty good job of letting it be assumed.'

'Well, I haven't decided yet.'

94

'Leaving it a bit late, aren't you?'

He shrugged with exaggerated nonchalance. 'There'll be time.' The truth was that he could not imagine any sort of future, could not conceive of it. His mind stopped at Schools and anything beyond was like speculating about someone else. He smiled at the thought that perhaps he suffered from the malaise which he attributed to Chetwynd: that nothing was real for him unless he had imagined it. It was the same with the baby; he had not imagined the possibility that it might be his and therefore had not yet absorbed it, had not made room for it. The idea was vivid but not credible. Even Anne's swollen shape added nothing to its reality.

There was a discussion between Anne and Dr Barry about shopping which ended with Anne's saying she wanted the walk and Dr Barry saying he wanted neither to come with her nor to leave her to carry the shopping home. He said he would go in the morning.

'I told you, I want the walk,' she said. 'Robert can come, if he's not in a hurry and doesn't mind being used as a pack mule.'

'Excellent idea,' said Dr Barry, his eyes twinkling at Robert. 'The rehearsal can wait, I'm sure.'

They walked to a small self-service shop newly opened in North Parade. She walked slowly and talked easily, asking him about the play, about Tim and Suzanne, Tim's money, Tim's BMW, what Tim intended to do. She heard his confession of the Jaguar with delighted incredulity and he received her admonitions with the pleasure he always took in being admonished by women.

While they talked he forgot for minutes at a time about the baby. Each time he made himself think of it he began to feel slightly sick but that did not last long. He would then feel that he had broken away into a floating inner region where nothing mattered. Things happened, that was all, first one thing, then another, until one day they would all stop and there would be nothing more to happen. What mattered now wouldn't matter then, and would go on not mattering for ever. So why should it matter now? One moment he was resigned, the next he wanted nothing more than to talk.

'Does David know?' he asked as they were waiting to cross the Woodstock Road.

'No.'

'How sure are you that it's — '

'I'm not at all sure.' She spoke sharply.

'I suppose he'd mind a lot. Understandably.' He had to repeat himself because a bus was passing.

She looked at him. 'Do you?'

'Yes.'

She continued looking. 'Do you?'

'Yes.' The repetition sounded unconvincing even to his own ears. 'We'd better cross at the zebra crossing.'

In the shop he followed behind her with the wire basket while she dithered over what to buy. Each contributed dutifully to a half-hearted conversation about Michael Mann.

Robert was aware of some disturbance at the checkout desk but was still paying attention only to Anne. When he looked towards the raised voices he saw the shop manager, two women assistants and Chetwynd. Chetwynd was remonstrating passionately, his thin face desperate. One of the women kept saying she would ring for the police. The manager, a plump worried man with glasses, repeated, 'Now let's get this straight,' again and again. The other woman held a folded green plastic mackintosh with a packet of tea on top.

Chetwynd's eyes were now on Robert, earnest and imploring. He looked older and smaller and his face more lined. Robert stared back, allowing himself to be implicated. For himself he did not care but he could sense Anne's puzzlement as she looked from one to the other.

Chetwynd pointed at him. 'If you really want to know, it's his,' he said. 'They're both his, the coat and the tea. We're friends and he asked me to hold them for him while

96

he helped his friend with her shopping. We were to meet here, by the checkout.'

They all looked at Robert. He paused before speaking slowly. 'That's right. I was just going to pick them up.'

The more vociferous of the women put her hand over the tea. 'If it's yours, tell us what it is.'

'It's tea, as he said.'

'What sort?'

'Twinings.'

'What did you give it to him for?'

'I was helping my friend with her shopping, as he told you. I didn't want my things mixed up with hers.'

The woman stared in angry disbelief. Anne took the basket from him and went back among the shelves.

Chetwynd turned to the man with more of his usual confidence. 'I tried to tell you, if only you'd listened. He has no more intention of not paying for the tea than I have of walking off with his coat.'

'Why didn't you say all this straight away?' demanded the woman.

Chetwynd smiled. 'I would have but you overwhelmed me.'

The manager looked relieved and shamefaced. 'Better give them back to him.'

The woman snatched the coat from her companion and looked at Robert. 'Not till he tells us what's in the pockets.'

Robert shrugged. 'I'll show you if you like but at this moment I couldn't tell you. So long since I wore it. No need with this weather.'

'Why were you carrying it, then?'

'I just picked it up from a friend.'

'Anything from this shop in the pockets?'

He sighed, to gain time. Chetwynd moved his head very slightly.

'No. Have a look if you don't believe me.'

They returned the coat and tea. Anne took her basket to the girl at the till and it was checked out in silence.

The manager went to the back of the shop, the quieter of the two women to the other till and the disbelieving one behind the meat counter. The other customers, who had been observing surreptitiously, carried on with their shopping.

By the time Robert had paid for the tea Anne was out of the shop. Chetwynd, carrying a plastic bag, held the door open for him.

'Can't thank you sufficiently so I won't try. I'll find a way.'

'Quick thinking on your part.'

'Yours, yours.'

Anne walked ahead but Chetwynd walked with exasperating slowness. 'Stupidity, mere stupidity. Always the little things that get you, the unconsidered trifles. I wasn't even after anything. Already had a packet of the stuff in my bag which I'd paid for. Went back and slipped the second under my coat more or less without thinking. Habit, you see. I love the feeling of getting something for nothing. They pounced too early, of course. Should have waited till I was out of the shop.'

Anne was drawing farther ahead. Robert handed him the mackintosh and the tea. Chetwynd insisted he kept the latter. 'I'll bring thanks when I see you next. Tell me about your woman then. She looks unhappy. You'll be blamed. It's always like that. Base your defence on compassion for me — hopeless case, string of juvenile convictions, nervous breakdown, widowed, two small children and so on. The child bit usually works.' He held out his hand. His eyes were moist. 'Look, I'm starting to shake now. Getting old for this. We shall meet soon.'

Chetwynd's hand was limp. Robert shook it lightly and then ran to catch Anne. He reached for the bag. 'I'll take that.'

'It's all right, it's not heavy.'

'Come on.' She let go easily, without looking at him. 'Sorry about all that.'

'It wasn't your fault.'

'I felt bad about it, you being there.'

'Why?'

'Dragging you into it like that.'

'Who was he?'

'Chetwynd. He's in college. I must have mentioned him. Reads Anglo-Saxon, mainly.'

'Is he a friend of yours?'

'Sort of. Mine as much as anyone's.'

She looked at him. 'Are you always as good as that to your friends?'

'Not much else I could do.'

'A lot of people wouldn't have.'

'Do you think I shouldn't have?'

She looked away. 'It's up to you what you do with your friends.'

Robert continued quickly. 'He often steals. He gets a kick out of it. But never anything serious, as far as I know.'

She gently touched his arm. 'Do you mind if we slow down a little? We're not running away now.'

He walked her to her front door and then, to avoid embarrassment, quickly said he had to be on his way. She asked where and he had to confess it was only back to college, adding, pointlessly, that he might decide to go out later. He was considering kissing her goodbye when she stepped inside.

'I'll call round again,' he said hastily.

She looked distracted. 'Yes, do, it would be nice, 'Bye.'

Chapter Six

The next rehearsal of *The Changeling* was in the loft of a building off Walton Street. It was ill-lit and dusty, with bare boards, no chairs and rough brickwork.

Everyone was present because it was to be a full run-through, though the building was too small. It would distort blocking and pace and make it difficult for the actors to project as if in a large auditorium, but Robert had insisted. He had no feel for the play as a whole, no idea of its shape, no idea how long it would take. When the cast gathered more or less punctually for once there was an air of excitement.

Even Gina was only a few minutes late. It was the first time he had seen her since asking her to undress. When he spoke to her about the blocking they were both quick and businesslike.

There was some nervous and unnecessary reading of scripts. As a concession to Malcolm, Robert organized exercises culminating in a wheelbarrow race which left everyone hot and ready. Only Gina did not join in.

They began early and finished late. It was patchy and untidy, too long by twenty minutes and very slow in the second act. The madhouse scenes were embarrassing. He had paid little attention to the sub-plot despite its theatrical possibilities and Michael Mann's warning. The neglect showed. Malcolm was better than before but still lacked conviction and intensity. The scene where De Flores presents Beatrice with the finger of Alonzo, whom he has murdered on her behalf, was not only unconvincing but funny. Yet it was probably the crucial scene

100

of the play, the moral and spiritual centre. Beatrice, forced to recognize in herself the evil she shares with De Flores, yields to his blackmail and his truth. If this was wrong everything was wrong. Robert watched it with an inward freezing despair.

Afterwards he went to Malcolm. He did not want to upset him but could not say nothing. 'We're going to have to do a lot more on the finger scene.'

'Really? I thought it went pretty well.'

'Lines like, "a woman dipped in blood, and talk of modesty?" have got to be right, otherwise they're just funny.'

'How should it be, then?'

'Less energetic. It should be slower.' He was going to say less hysterical but sensed Malcolm was too near that already.

'Really? How? Can you show me?'

Malcolm's tone was flip and jaunty, as unconvincing as his acting. 'Show me,' he said again. 'If you're so sure about it, do it.'

Robert did not want to demonstrate. He doubted that he could do it very well. Neither did he want a confrontation, though at the same time he was reluctant to back down. The others were looking on. He smiled. 'If I knew how to take the hero's part, I would.'

'I'm surprised that stops you.'

It was a public challenge. It was absurd to have got into this position so easily. He was as angry with himself as with Malcolm.

'He'd run a mile if he had to play the hero,' said Gina, good-naturedly. 'Even without an audience.'

Some of the others smiled. She asked Malcolm something about the blocking and he started to explain to her. The danger passed.

The publicity man appeared with the next round of posters which were due to go up the following day. Designed by someone from Ruskin, they showed a man's and a woman's face side by side and merging into each other, each in white and peopled by miniature black madmen and courtiers. Everyone liked them and there was a scramble for copies to keep.

Gina had a canvas bag for her books. Robert went to her while she was making room in it for the folded poster. Malcolm and most of the others had gone.

'Thank you. That was getting awkward.'

'It'll be more awkward if you don't do something about it.'

'Perhaps I should speak to him alone. He's less likely to bridle then.' She picked up her bag. 'With him like that there's no sense of deadly kinship between the two of you.'

She raised her eyebrows. 'Deadly kinship?'

He again felt that she was laughing at him and so smiled as if he had meant to be funny. 'You were very good.'

'Thank you.'

'Almost too good. I hope you won't go off the boil before first night.'

'Don't worry about that.' She hitched her bag over her shoulder and left.

Robert climbed into bed that night feeling drained. Everything seemed to demand of him though he suspected that at bottom he demanded everything of himself. His concerns were real enough, they existed, yet they felt like diversions. He avoided asking himself from what.

The play had begun like a love affair in which all seemed possible, then the drudgery of rehearsal took over and the original inspiration fragmented into a hundred petty concerns, none so petty as not to demand his attention. He knew now with despairing certainty that it would not work as it should but all he could do was to trudge stubbornly on, hoping without hope that what had inspired him would still somehow be bodied forth on the stage. Then there was the quiet cancer of Schools, now another day closer, another day without his opening a

102

book. Thoughts of Anne and the baby brought sharper pains but, unlike Schools, there was no finality about them, they led nowhere. He was no more sure about what he felt than about what he wanted. He did not trust his own reactions to anything.

He longed more for respite than for sleep. It was as if he had been wrestling with something for so many years that he no longer knew how to stop. As sleep crept over him he heard his own voice asking aloud which way he should go. An answering voice, not his own, spoke his name and asked which way he wanted.

He woke instantly and lay in the dark with his heart beating fast. It had been a glancing touch, the brush of a wing, no more. He waited vainly for something else. The curtains over the small window were light and still in the darkness. He got up and looked out. There was no moon and the rooftops were jumbled and angular. A maverick bell chimed once. He sat in his armchair in darkness and silence, waiting, but nothing happened. Then he thought that nothing would happen, that it was for him to initiate. He switched on the light, sat at his desk and rapidly completed the application for the theological college. He returned to bed fully awake yet more at peace now than for months and fell quickly into a deep dreamless sleep.

It was still with him the next morning, a cleansing sense of calm and purpose. He determined to work and gathered together his Old Testament books. It was easier than the New; the Yahweh of the Old was an acceptable mystery, but the God of the New was a demand for which few were ready. To love and obey meant a revolution in oneself and hardly anyone wanted that, any more than they wanted to give everything away or love their neighbours. He would come to that later, perhaps.

He sorted out his essays, put them by the books, then sat staring before reassembling everything into a neat pile. A change of scene was needed. Robert often said he was oblivious to his surroundings and certainly he made no attempt to impose his personality upon his room. There

103

was no decoration of any sort, his clothes were jumbled in a trunk in the corner, his books stacked on the floor. He spent so little time there that it was hard not to suspect that it depressed him. Yet it was clear that he liked homeliness. He would sit and talk in other people's rooms for hours, especially Tim's. Sometimes he claimed he lacked the homely touch, at others that he could not be bothered.

There was a note on his door to call Tim. It was unlike Tim to be up so early but Robert found him sitting barefoot in his armchair drinking tea and reading the *New Yorker* by the subdued light of his brass table lamp. His stereo system was playing a recording of bird song which he always said was better than anything nature could produce.

Tim pointed at the mantelpiece. 'Chetwynd's been in already. Said he couldn't rouse you. Left you that.'

It was a reproduction of a seventeenth-century French painting in which two red-haired, bare-breasted sisters were at their toilette. One tweaked the other's nipple while in the other hand she held a wedding ring, her fingers forming an identical gesture.

'Said he owed you a favour,' continued Tim. 'Said he'd paid for it too. Tea?'

Robert shook his head. 'I'm going to work.'

'Really, or are you just trying to make me feel bad?'

'Go and count the gargoyles.'

Tim sat with the empty cup in his lap. He held the big teapot waveringly in one hand. 'How are Dr and Mrs Barry?'

'Well, well.'

'My, my.' He poured the tea shakily. 'With you working I'm going to have to think of something else to do.' Some of the tea missed the cup but he continued pouring and grinning. 'It's hot, you know, really hot. I am in real pain.'

Robert left the painting where it was and headed for the Bodleian. The college library was nearer but he wanted to walk. It was already hot.

He went to Duke Humfrey's Room in the Old Bodleian,

104

where he had first seen Anne. It was cool and quiet, smelling of old volumes and old wood. By Oxford standards it was still early and there were plenty of empty desks. He set out his books and papers and again studied them for a few minutes before deciding to go to George's Café in the covered market for coffee and a read of the paper. Then he would get down to work. He had had no breakfast and, having established a place in the library, he felt it possible to go elsewhere with an easier conscience. Days had passed like that.

The covered market was a bustling cheerful place where butchers displayed hanging game and stuffed animals and where the smell of ground coffee spread everywhere from a shop in the corner. George's sold tea and sweet Camp coffee in large mugs. The walls were covered by posters of plays, concerts and meetings. It was filled in the mornings by working people having what some still called their elevenses and by undergraduates at breakfast.

He was passing the grocer's when he saw Suzanne. Looking at her dark hair and quick pale features again, he began to see Tim's point. She smiled when she saw him — 'showing the gap' was what Tim called it. 'You look as if you've just fallen out of bed,' she said.

'Coffee in George's. Want some?'

Her features showed struggle. 'All right, if it's quick. Liz is giving a dinner party and I'm doing some of her shopping because she's got an essay crisis. I'll join you there.'

Waiting for her was one of the few periods in the last year or so when he felt he had some control over his life. He had deliberately created a situation in which he now had choice. He could either do what he ought — work — or do something quite different. The thought was mildly exhilarating, though he recognized the element of self-deceit. He had been making the choice without acknowledging it for most of the past year. He was making it now.

When Suzanne came she pushed up the sleeves of her

loose white blouse and held her mug of coffee in both hands. She talked of a summer holiday in Greece. He remembered Tim saying she had told him she did not know what she was going to do.

'Tim's coming to see you this morning,' he said, spontaneously changing what he had been thinking. 'He's probably on his way now. He's going to suggest a pub lunch in Wytham and a walk.'

She smiled and shook her head. 'I must work. Anyway, I told him I wouldn't see him till after Schools.'

'He's asked me, too. We're going in the new car I've got. Old car, rather. It won't take long. We've all got Schools. We can all work first.'

She put down her coffee and sat back. 'The disarming thing about you, Robert, is you're so obvious.'

'What d'you mean?'

'Well, I could button up my blouse or sit at another table. Whichever makes you more comfortable.'

'I can see you better as you are.'

She laughed and pushed back her hair with both hands. 'I suppose I could work this evening instead. I wasn't going to.'

Books lay open on Tim's desk but he was on his knees with a screwdriver doing something to one of the stereo speakers. His coffee apparatus was gurgling. He took the news with a resigned grin and tossed the screwdriver into the air, watching it fall point first on to Ryle's *Concept of the Mind*.

'So now it takes someone else to chat up my woman for me. She wouldn't have said yes if it had been just me.'

'Perhaps she doesn't realize she's your woman.'

'Not much chance she's going to find out with you there.'

'I'll push off by myself while you two go for a walk. I'll take a book.'

'Very convincing.' He got up and retrieved the screw-

106

driver. 'Why don't we take the BMW? I don't trust your Jag. I was listening to it when the bloke delivered it.'

'I want to try it out. Anyway, I've got to move it. It's in the dons' car park.'

'If it moves.'

There was still time to work. To help fill it Robert went to the porter's lodge but there was only a letter from home. It was in his father's carefully sloping handwriting, asking if he had heard from the theological college. The vicar, who had sent a reference, had been asking after him. The vicar had said again that they should be very proud of him and had told his mother that they should travel down to see him get his degree. When would that be? His father would need to know so that he could get the day off.

Robert pushed the letter hurriedly into the back pocket of his jeans. His father would have written it painstakingly on the kitchen table between tea and the television news and would have posted it when he started work at five the next morning. Robert pushed it deeper into his pocket, as if to stifle it. Letters from home brought with them an unbearable sadness and sweetness, an innocence that made him tender and hopeless.

As he turned to go he saw Hansford peering over the top of the letter rack, the only man in college who could.

'Robert.'

'What?'

Hansford indicated by facial contortion that he wished to speak outside. In the quad he took Robert by the arm and led him to the shade. 'Seen Orpwood today or heard anything?'

'No.' Robert was anxious to get to work now.

'They're planning something.'

'Aren't they always?'

'This is different. That Iraqi chap's speaking at the Union tonight. We're demonstrating against it — peacefully, of course. I think they're planning a bit of violent disruption.'

107

'Well, the police will be there.'

'No, more personal than that. Look what I found in my pigeon-hole.' He held out a piece of lined paper on which was written in untidy print, HANSFORD IS A FACIST. POLITICAL DINOSAURS REMEMBER MUSSOLINI.

Robert was thinking that it might take time to start the Jaguar. The battery wasn't very good. 'Dinosaurs lasted much longer than we have. Nothing to worry about if that's what they think of you.'

'But they're mad, this lot. They don't know about the dinosaurs. They only know about the meat hook.'

'Childish malice.'

Hansford shook his head. 'Children are vicious.'

He wanted Robert to examine the handwriting but Robert said he had to rush and promised to keep his eyes open. He was stopped after a few yards by Hansford's voice, now at normal volume.

'You haven't by any chance lost your bike, have you? Had it pinched or anything?'

Robert put his hand to his head. 'I'd forgotten about that. Lent it to someone the other day and can't remember who.'

'It's blue, isn't it? Straight handlebars and no mudguards, with a broken saddle and the three-speed whatsit hanging off?'

'Sounds about right. Where is it?'

'Down near the station. I'm going down there. I'll bring it back. I can wheel it alongside mine while I'm riding.'

'You sure?'

'No problem. See you.'

Hansford mounted his own bike, which he made look small and frail. Robert waved goodbye. He always felt guilty for not liking Hansford more and because of that pretended to like him more than he did.

In winter the White Hart was quiet and had a fire but in summer it was hard to get even a seat in the garden. They made do with a low wall. Suzanne and Tim had salad, Robert his usual pie and beans.

'Didn't you say you were going to wash your hands?' she asked.

'Oh, yes.' He went to the gents and tried to get the oil off. The battery had been low, as expected, and the carburetters had flooded. He'd had to take out the plugs and dry them, then had been further delayed by an altercation with the Domestic Bursar about parking places. He had had to feign contrition. On the way Tim had calmly remarked that it wasn't firing on all cylinders.

'Can't do any better without Vim or Swarfega,' he said, rejoining them.

'It's nice here. It was a good idea.' She smiled and looked at them both. 'Whose ever it was.'

'Better without all these people. Makes you want to machine-gun them.'

'That's very sweet of you. Sorry — men don't like being called sweet, do they?'

'He's just had to be nice to the Bursar,' said Tim.

'Poor thing.' She talked about the history of Wytham. Tim said that each time anyone told him about Oxfordshire he resolved to learn something for himself and that he also made the same remark each time.

The conversation was pleasant but dissatisfying, as if they were skirting the issue. Robert had no precise idea what the issue was, only an urge to say or do something decisive or get away. He noticed for the first time how much Suzanne moved her shoulders when she spoke, so that they seemed to rise and fall with the stress patterns in her sentences. He looked at her as if she were at rehearsal. Tim made little effort, seemingly content with his salad, but his silences betrayed tension and self-consciousness. Robert was about to say that he would go off and read while they walked when Suzanne abruptly stopped speaking. They both looked at her.

'You're neither of you listening to a word I'm saying,' she said. 'What are you thinking about?'

109

Tim smiled insincerely. 'I was thinking of Horace Walpole's, "This world is a comedy to those that think, a tragedy to those that feel." '

Suzanne sat back and laughed helplessly. One hand shielded her eyes against the sun, the other held her stomach as if in pain. When she recovered she lent forward and touched his arm. 'I'm sorry, but you're so funny when you're trying to be serious.'

Tim continued to smile. 'I was wondering about the feelers who ceased to feel.'

'No one ceases to feel.'

'You think not?'

'Of course not. They just feel differently.' She stood. 'I'll get another drink.'

Tim stood. 'I'll get it.'

She took the glasses. 'You can't be profound and masterful at the same time. You'll give me hiccoughs.'

Afterwards the three of them wandered up the lane towards the woods. Robert took Heaton's *The Hebrew Kingdoms*, saying he would go off by himself and read in a field. Before they reached the bend, though, the quiet was shattered by a black Ford Escort with lowered suspension, wide wheels, darkened windows and an oversized exhaust. It roared up behind them and shot past within inches of Robert's arm. The tyres squealed on the corner as it accelerated out of sight. Tim swore, something he very rarely did.

When they rounded the bend they saw the car turning at the top of the hill. It stopped for a minute or two, then started rapidly back down towards them.

'It's coming back, the horrible thing,' Suzanne said and stepped to the side of the road.

Robert was about to follow but saw that Tim had not. Tim's narrowed gaze was fixed on the car. Robert did not attempt to catch his eye but stayed beside him. He sensed in Tim a careless indifference and himself felt a sudden excitement. The car was suddenly much closer. Suzanne said something but the two of them continued walking.

110

The car flashed its lights. Robert looked up from the glare to the sky. Tim looked straight ahead.

There was another loud squeal and the car skidded to the side, almost into the ditch. When Robert looked again there was still smoke coming from its tyres. Inside were two young men and he realized there might be a fight. He didn't want that, his initial anger was gone, so he stared at the car as if he might want a fight. Tim continued walking with the same determined, blank expression as before. From close-to Robert could see that the men were very young, perhaps no more than seventeen. They did not look pugnacious. The driver scowled and made a V-sign through the windscreen, then drove off more slowly.

They walked on without speaking until the sound had died away.

'What was that supposed to prove?' Suzanne asked quietly.

Robert glanced at Tim. 'I think we were angry with them.'

'You might have died.'

'We shall anyway,' said Tim.

'They were dangerous,' Robert added.

She looked away. 'It's you two that are dangerous.'

Robert finally left them at the top of the hill, insisting against Suzanne's protestations of disbelief that he really was going to read.

Tim and Suzanne went on across the field at the top and strolled into the green depths of the woods. There were high beech trees, each a towering, spreading, many-levelled universe. The trunks were massive and smooth, the boughs strong and gentle. The tallest thing in man's kingdom and a sensible thing to worship, Tim thought; had there been anything he wanted to worship. Suzanne talked about the natural history research that was done in the woods and pointed to the nets, markers, wire baskets and other contraptions. Tim was interested.

They circled back towards Wytham and came into a

high field where Tim climbed the barbed-wire fence with the aid of a branch, then helped her over, keeping hold of her hand. The wood was behind them and on either side. Before them the field sloped steeply at first, levelling off towards the village. Highland cattle, red, shaggy, wide-horned beasts, grazed near the priory at the bottom. Beyond were the towers and spires of Oxford, dominated now by modern buildings. The heat was aggressive.

He found a patch that looked clear of thistles and suggested they sat. When they lay down she let him kiss her. They looked solemnly into each other's eyes and, finding nothing to say, kissed again. He lay back on the grass. the warm weight of her head on his arm. the sun hot on his eyelids. The grass was prickly.

They dozed briefly and he had a succession of vivid and confusing dreams. When he opened his eyes he had to close them immediately because of the brilliance of the sky. He kissed her again. She responded at first but when he put the tip of his tongue between the gap in her teeth her body stiffened and she moved her head away.

'Do you want us to get out of the field?' he asked.

She squinted against the sun. 'No.'

'What, then?'

'I don't trust you.'

'Why not?'

She sat up and shook her hair. 'Do you think Robert's really reading?'

She had never been subtle about not answering questions, tending simply to look away and change the subject. He could imagine her as a little girl doing the same with precocious seriousness. 'No idea.' He lay on his back again, feeling suddenly hopeless. 'Do you fancy him?'

'He's fanciable, I suppose, in some ways, but not for me. Why?'

'You talk about him.'

She smiled. 'I talk about you but what does that mean?'

112

'Would you have come today if it had been just me inviting you?'

She turned away and sat with her arms around her knees, staring down at the priory. 'The trouble is, you never discuss ideas.'

'What do you mean? What ideas?'

'You're not intellectual. I don't mean you're not intelligent. You're just not intellectually interested.'

The accusation must have stung him because he mentioned it later more than once. He seemed to feel that the lack she spoke of was not merely intellectual. At the time he remarked facetiously that Shakespeare, too, never discussed ideas.

She look irritated. 'It's intellectual stimulation that makes me want to make love with someone. That's what excites me.' He mentioned platonic love and laughed. She looked more irritated. 'There's something about you and Robert, something missing. Like with that car.'

After leaving them Robert had walked in a wide semi-circle back towards the village. He had not stopped to read but had kept planning to stop at places still ahead of him, changing his mind once there and carrying on with the walk. He again had the teasing sense of choice — that he could stop whenever he liked, if only he chose — and again the sense of a choice already made.

Eventually he headed for the churchyard by the priory. The priory was a stone building, long since converted into flats. Behind it was a large, low-walled garden and beyond and upwards stretched the high fields that Tim and Suzanne were lying in. Before it was a gravelled yard used as a car park and path to the church. As Robert was crossing the yard the big priory door opened and Dr Barry came out with the Bursar's secretary. She was a short, lively girl whom he did not at first recognize in jeans and a flimsy pink blouse. He and Dr Barry saw each other immediately. Dr Barry looked thrown for a moment, shifty and almost fearful. He glanced down, then up

113

again, his quick eyes and smile now prepared. Robert remembered that the Bursar's secretary had a flat in the priory.

'Surprise, surprise,' Dr Barry said. 'And a book in hand, too.'

It was the Bursar's secretary who looked the more surprised. She smiled diffidently.

'I was going to read in the churchyard,' said Robert.

Dr Barry said something about an elegy and he and the girl both laughed.

Robert smiled, to show he was not ill-disposed. He felt calm and unassailable.

Dr Barry looked about as if he had just arrived. 'Beautiful, isn't it?'

'It is, yes.'

'Ideal for a drink and a walk.'

'That's what I thought.'

'It's worth the journey,' said the Bursar's secretary. 'Much better than staying in town.'

They walked over to Dr Barry's Ford. Dr Barry got in while she stood with her arms folded. Robert resumed his walk towards the church. As the car drew away the Bursar's secretary waved goodbye once, briefly, then hurried back inside. Robert caught Dr Barry's eye, unsmiling. Now Barry raised one hand from the wheel, as if in acknowledgement.

Robert did not mention the meeting to Tim and Suzanne when they returned. The Jaguar started easily but would not idle and twice stalled at traffic lights. Suzanne insisted on sitting in the back but talked most of the time whereas Tim, apart from an occasional comment, was mostly silent. He became more lively, however, after she had put her hand on his shoulder to explain something.

As they drew up outside St Hilda's they saw Orpwood dodging between the parked cars. He had an armful of Stop the War leaflets advertising the meeting at the Union that night and was placing them under windscreen wipers. He moved quickly, stooping and furtive. He approached the Jaguar without at first realizing there was someone in it.

When he saw them he stopped. 'You don't mind one, do you? They're not stick-on, so they don't mess up the windscreen.' His eyes flickered across to Suzanne.

'I do, yes. I've just bought it,' said Robert.

'It's yours, is it? Looks a bit flash for you.' He stood back admiringly. 'Does it use much petrol?'

'I don't know. Probably.'

The door opened and shut. Suzanne was already on the pavement. 'It's horribly flash and he can't afford it. Thanks for a lovely lunch, both of you. Don't crash it on the way back. Bye.' She kissed Tim on the cheek through the open window then walked quickly through the gates.

'Couldn't give me a lift back to college, could you?' asked Orpwood. 'I'm more or less finished here.' He got in. 'They go a bit, these things, don't they? My brother-in-law's got a new one. Right capitalist fat-cat but it's a great car. You coming to the meeting tonight?'

They both said they were not.

'Should be lively. The fascists are planning a demo and the pigs will be out in force.'

'Sounds like a confrontation situation,' said Tim laconically.

Orpwood nodded seriously. 'We hope it will be. It's all to our advantage, see, even if we get beaten up. Contributes to the breakdown of law and order.'

'That's what you want, is it? So you can replace it with your own law and order?' Tim spoke now with unusual sharpness.

'Well, that's over-simplifying it, but yes. You're not interested in all this, are you? I thought you two were apolitical.'

'Are there any apoliticals in your terms?'

'Not really, they're all right-wing.'

They stopped at the traffic lights by Magdalen. Robert

115

turned and grinned. 'Ought you to be seen in a car like this with us?'

Orpwood laughed harshly, as if he lacked practice. 'No one will look for me in it. Who was that girl?'

'Suzanne Walker. Does history.'

'Not bad, is she?'

'Not bad.'

'You seem to get around with the women, Robert.'

'It's Tim who gets around with her.'

Tim gazed out of the window. 'Could've fooled me.'

Orpwood continued unabashed. 'Wish I had more time, really, but it's difficult when you're politically involved. Then there's work, of course.'

He was convulsed by a hay-feverish sort of sneeze. It occurred to Robert that he was probably one of the many virgin men in Oxford. 'What about Jan Simpson? You must see quite a bit of her.'

Orpwood shook his head quickly. 'Difficult with people you see a lot of. Then there's the time problem.'

'Yes, the time problem,' Robert murmured.

Chapter Seven

Robert was early and stood alone in the seeming vastness of the Newman Rooms. *The Changeling* was allowed an extra rehearsal because *Marat-Sade* had had to close. He contemplated the litter of scaffolding, chairs, props and flats left by the failed production and for the first time was seriously frightened. It seemed impossible that the scrappy bits of rehearsal could ever come together in a coherent whole, that the blocking and lighting would work, that the set would not be dwarfed, that people should pay to come in and stay until the end. He wished he were somewhere far away where no one knew him.

He paced slowly in the gloom, his notes under his arm. By not switching on the lights he kept the world from him for a while. The props for *Marat-Sade* lay all over the floor. The production had ended in such confusion and hopelessness that no one had been in all day to clear up. People said the lunatic scenes were abysmal. Thinking of that made his stomach feel hollow.

He sensed rather than heard a presence and turned to see Gina sitting on the upturned bath used in *Marat-Sade*. She had drawn up her knees and was resting her chin on them, watching. It was just possible to make out that she was smiling.

'I didn't know you were here. Were you here when I came in?' His voice sounded rudely loud.

'I followed you in. Don't worry, you didn't talk to yourself.'

'It's unlike you to be early.'

'And you.'

117

He sat on the other end of the bath. 'I can't see how it will work in here. It could be a nightmare.'

'You chose to dream.'

'But it's so big and there's so little time.' He was relieved to talk. 'It frightens me.'

'Do you regret doing it?'

'Not quite. Not yet.'

'There might be more problems with Malcolm. I saw him this afternoon. He was fractious.'

'Well, it was you that got us through it last time. You may have to do it again.' She turned her head away as he looked at her. He noticed how small and white her clasped hands were. 'It's like being in church here,' he added.

She gave a short soft laugh. 'Is there something you want to confess?'

The door banged open, there were voices and lights. Antonio and Franciscus appeared; others were locking bikes. Lollis had an essay crisis and wanted to leave early. Malcolm had sent a message saying he would be late. The lights man said his plan was hopeless, the new set designer was despondent, the stage manager frantic. Robert cajoled, persuaded, bullied, postponed, brought forward, abandoned, inspired, decided.

Once rehearsal was under way he spared neither himself nor the cast. They had by now developed a group personality. He could sense a growing appetite for recognition and independence, though there was still a deep desire to be led and a leader who did not lead would be destroyed. He tried to keep one step ahead by demanding more than they expected to give, which entailed pretending to more confidence and purpose than he had.

The trouble with Malcolm began with the lines following the stabbing of Alonzo. He was overly dramatic and theatrical and they had to go through the scene four times. Malcolm became tired, querulous and brittle. Robert stopped him half way through the fifth. 'Still too mannered. You should be thinking aloud, telling us your

118

thoughts, not making a speech up about them. Stop haranguing. You're not playing Mark Anthony.'

The last remark was careless. Malcolm threw up his hands and turned with the very staginess Robert had been criticizing. 'All right, if you're so bloody marvellous you do it. Show us.' Everyone was silent. Robert sat with his elbows on his knees and his notes spread on the floor between his feet. He was weary of everything. He would have liked to walk out and bother with nothing, not the play, not Schools, not whether he lived or died. Instead, he spoke as reasonably as he could.

'I can't, Malcolm, I'm no good. But you can. That's why you're doing it. Have another go.'

Malcolm folded his arms and glanced at the others for support. 'Not till you demonstrate. You've got such a clear idea you must be able to demonstrate. I'm sure you want to, don't you, rather than sit there and criticize?'

Robert did not want to. If he did badly Malcolm would be jubilant; if he did well, pride would prevent Malcolm from emulating him, even if he could. But the point was to get the play done. If he were to do anything at all it had to be that. He got up slowly.

Everyone stood back. Malcolm's smile was mocking but uneasy. The murdered Alonzo, who had been squatting on the floor, lay down again. Robert told him to get up. 'We'll take the scene from the beginning, where De Flores lets you in.'

He did not know all of De Flores's lines but was fairly confident of this and the next scene with Beatrice. They went through his welcoming of Alonzo, his relieving him of his sword and then stabbing him three times. The disputed lines followed the stabbing but Robert stopped when he reached them.

'Let's do the stabbing again. I'd lost momentum.'

He threw himself into it. After sitting and watching for so long, action and movement were exhilarating. When it came to the disputed lines, those accompanying the severing of the dead Alonzo's finger, he was already

119

breathless. It was easy and natural to do them as if thinking aloud.

He could tell from the faces of the others that it was at least not bad. To his surprise, he had enjoyed it. He felt good. 'Like that,' he said to Malcolm. Malcolm's face was tense and livid. 'You don't need me, then.'

'Of course we do.'

'Well, you can do without.'

Malcolm turned and walked quickly towards the door, tripping against the bath on his way. Robert did not call after him. He would see him tomorrow, tell him how much he was needed, flatter and coax him, whatever was necessary. The thing now was to get on with it.

'Act Three, Scene Three,' he said crisply. 'I'll play De Flores in Scene Four.' The outer doors banged shut. They went through the second scene again, twice through the third then moved on to the fourth. This was the crucial scene with Gina in which Malcolm had given trouble before. Acting opposite her was something Robert had often thought about but never expected. It was quite different from talking to her, not because she became another person but because she was Gina concentrated, distilled, no longer diffused by social context. She was by turn ambivalent and intense, not distracting from the words she spoke but seeming to inhabit them indefinably, like mist among trees. It was the words and it was her; the two could not be separated.

Robert fumbled his lines and several times had to start again. He tried to be harder on himself than he had been on Malcolm, getting the others to criticize him. He did not know the play as well as he thought.

As they went on he realized why Malcolm was so reluctant to look at Gina on stage. Hers was a daunting acting intelligence, powerful, flashing, swift as a blade. Malcolm's defence had been to avert his eyes and try to act his own part independently. Robert realized he had to engage her fully in order not to be overwhelmed. He devoured her with his eyes, his movements he made predatory, his manner calculating and passionate. He felt her respond and when, twice, she had to prompt him she did it softly and quickly as if as keen as he to continue.

Afterwards he felt both drained and excited. He went over to her. 'Sorry. I thought I knew it better than I did.' He wanted her to say something complimentary.

'Same time tomorrow?'

'Yes.'

'I might be a few minutes late.' She picked up her bag.

'It's tiring, isn't it? Takes it out of you.'

She smiled as she walked away. 'Don't worry, you were all right. Better than Malcolm.'

It was a balmy night. Old Tom chimed sonorously in Christ Church tower. For a moment Robert thought he had forgotten his bike. He felt like a walk and headed up towards Carfax.

There was a police van parked and several policemen standing around outside the Union building. Robert was not a member, unlike Tim who sometimes slept in the leather armchairs in the library or took solitary tea in the Gladstone Room. As Robert approached he decided he would try to get in, less because he wanted to hear the debate than because he was excluded. He felt restless and unready for sleep. All the entrances would be guarded and so he walked to the main door. There was a desk just inside where passes were to be shown.

A man and a girl he knew slightly came out and he greeted them with unusual effusiveness. Someone at the desk asked for his pass but he pretended not to hear. He asked the couple whether it was worth his while going in, what had happened so far, who had spoken, whom they had seen in the audience.

While they were talking one of the policemen came in and addressed the officials at the desk. Robert walked on through. He climbed the stairs to the gallery, which was so packed he had to push his way forward to see the floor.

There was an air of excitement but it felt like excitement caused by something that had happened already, like goals at a football match. On the floor below a dark-haired serious-looking man with glasses was listening expressionlessly to the present speaker, a woman from a part of the hall Robert could not see. He assumed the man was the Iraqi. The woman was declaiming stridently about the Zionist-American axis. He pushed further forward and saw it was Jan Simpson. Her face looked paler than normal in the bright lights and her cropped brown hair shone with recent washing. He looked for Orpwood but recognized only Hansford, who was wearing a smart three-piece suit with a gold watch chain and was whispering to the man next to him. Someone said the press and radio had been there but had left after the Iraqi's speech. It was hot and people shifted uncomfortably.

Jan Simpson's voice was shrill and determined. She shouted small squads of words, pausing after each volley as she built up to her climax.

'The only peace is socialist peace! Peace is impossible with capitalism. Capitalism means oppression. Capitalism is inherently racist. In the Middle East and everywhere. We have our central heating and our comfortable cars. Millions have no food. But the day is coming soon when the people will rise up. They will demand rights for all people. Freedom and equality! Capitalism is against the march of history. It is doomed. It must not and cannot survive. It must and shall be destroyed. As long as one person is oppressed we are all in chains. We must fight, fight, fight!'

Her young face was white and excited. After a pause she continued in a lower key. Robert had begun to push his way out when he noticed a man hunched over the balcony at the front, apparently in rapt attention, his elbows on the rail and his head in his hands. Disturbed by the movement, the man glanced round and Robert saw it was Chetwynd. Chetwynd raised both eyebrows,

122

making a face as if he were doing a comic turn, and beckoned with his head. As Robert pushed his way down Jan Simpson was interrupted by one of Hansford's group who objected that she had strayed from the subject of the motion. Robert and Chetwynd were squeezed shoulder to shoulder.

'This is wonderful,' whispered Chetwynd. 'Absolute sincerity, inoperable naïvety. That once was me. I weep for my lost innocence. As if our wonderful workers would lift one fat finger to get themselves less heating and worse cars, poor deluded bitch. I could listen to her all night.'

'What was the Iraqi like?'

'Predictable press-fodder. This is the best bit because it shows what's really at issue, step by step, personal guilt to generalised guilt to intolerance to totalitarianism. Shows it, doesn't say it. They don't know they're doing it.'

Jan Simpson was concluding with a passionate appeal for peace, socialism and disarmament. 'I'm going,' said Robert. 'See you.'

Chetwynd grabbed his arm. 'Will you support me if I speak? I don't mean second me, I mean physically. I want to stand on the balcony. Will you hang on to me?'

'What do you want to say?'

'Anything, everything, the word is with me tonight. Are you my friend?' He gripped Robert's arm hard. His brown eyes shone and he grinned with feigned mania.

'All right, but don't get right up or I shan't be able to hold you.'

The man next to Hansford was preparing to speak. Chetwynd clambered hurriedly on to the balcony. He got one knee up, then the other foot, gripped Robert round the shoulders and raised his other arm theatrically. Robert held him by the forearm and hips, like a rugby player holding a team-mate aloft. The side of his face was pressed hard enough against Chetwynd's corduroys for him to feel the bony thigh.

'One law for the Lion and the Ox is oppression!'

123

Chetwynd shouted in a very deep voice, his arm still held high. 'Equality for all is the oppression of each!'

There was silence. The floor became rows of upturned faces and the people nearest him and Robert pushed themselves back. 'The marriage of equality and freedom is the great lie of our time. There's only one just system — the individual for his own sake. The common good equals common oppression. Every murderer's excuse for genocide!'

He fired off his words like shot in exaggerated imitation of Jan Simpson.

'Who talks of *the* people has contempt for people. Who loves the masses hates the individual. The socialist pulse beats to a totalitarian heart. Behind this lady's call to freedom is the will to power. Politics is love of power. The more political, the more power.'

Waving his free arm made him wobble and he had to clutch Robert's shoulder tightly, almost dragging him forward. After the first shock of the interruption people began to protest. The President called for order, Jan Simpson stared, one of her friends shouted something, one of Hansford's shouted something back. The Iraqi gazed with the same lack of expression as before.

Chetwynd looked down at Robert. 'Okay for round two?'

There was more shouting from the floor. People were on their feet, kicking their chairs back. Some called for Chetwynd to shut up or get out, others called for order. Chetwynd leaned dangerously far forward and Robert braced himself against the balcony. 'Two kinds of people!' shouted Chetwynd. 'Those who love others — those who hate and fear them. Haters love ideology. Who defines man ideologically hates and fears what he is. To categorize is to control, to control to deny. The essence of socialism is the desire to control. That is the sum of all your creeds!'

He bellowed the last sentence against growing protest. The debate had broken up. People tried to get down the stairs from the gallery while others tried to get up.

124

Chetwynd bent his face to Robert. 'This is orgiastic! Can you stand round three?'

'Don't move about so much.' Robert braced himself again and once more Chetwynd leaned forward. He was greeted by uproar from below. He waved his arm defiantly, his knee slipped and he toppled over. Robert was jerked so far forward that he could feel himself following. He held Chetwynd by his corduroys and one arm. Chetwynd swayed wildly, one hand on the balcony, the other round Robert's neck.

There were gasps from below and Chetwynd's legs flailed as he struggled for leverage. Robert, his eyes tight shut, pushed his knees against the balcony and tried to heave back. The muscles of his right arm quivered and he could feel his grip slipping. Chetwynd now had him by the hair. He clenched his teeth, gripped and heaved, but Chetwynd's struggles made it worse. He knew he could not go on. He would either have to let go or be pulled over. The corduroys seemed to burn his fingers. For a moment he thought he really was going over but then Chetwynd got one foot back on the ledge. After a few seconds he got greater purchase with an elbow and a knee. Robert heaved once more but too much this time. Chetwynd's weight came on top of him and they both tumbled to the floor of the gallery, panting and sweating. There was a great cheer.

Robert had banged his head on a bench and felt weak and shaky. 'Told you not to bloody wave,' he gasped.

Chetwynd grimaced. 'Your knee is in my crotch. Don't do anything. Let me move first.'

They disentangled carefully and got up. The confusion below had increased. The 'Stop the War' chant began, opposed by some uncoordinated heckling.

'I intended only a gesture,' said Chetwynd. 'This is a bonus.'

When they went to leave they found people jammed like tea leaves on the narrow stairs. Some slapped Chetwynd on the back. Others stared. Most made room.

'Anonymity from now on,' Chetwynd continued. 'Police make me nervous. I'll use the window rather than risk being mobbed in the street. Thanks for your support.'

Chetwynd had the vanishing knack and Robert soon lost sight of him. People streamed out into the street where two mobs had formed. They were chanting at each other, separated — quite acceptably to both, it appeared — by the police. Robert took the exit which led by a narrow passage to St Aldate's.

As he squeezed through the door he saw Suzanne and David Long in the crowd a few yards ahead. Her dark hair caught his eye and he could tell by the movement of her head that she was laughing. He could neither move back nor closer, but was forced to keep pace with them. They looked as if they might be holding hands.

When she reached the end of the alley she turned to face Robert, as abruptly as if someone had called her. She half smiled, made to turn back, then smiled fully before turning again and continuing.

Once in St Aldate's he stood with his back against the wall but he had lost sight of her. She would head down towards Carfax. It would be easy to catch her and speak but he didn't want that. He stared at the receding heads, stared obstinately until rewarded by a glimpse, a flash of her eyes from across the road. When he left he felt something of the sadness he had felt on finding Dr Barry with the Bursar's secretary.

Back at college he found Hansford at the bottom of Tim's staircase, apparently doing nothing. 'Come and see what they've done,' said Hansford as if continuing rather than beginning a conversation.

They went up to his room, which was lit by a single bulb suspended from the ceiling. The lampshade was dented and tilted, two of the four window panes were broken and glass and papers were scattered across the desk and floor.

'See what I mean? I knew they'd do something. I said so, do you remember? They've got it in for me.'

'Orpwood and his crowd?'

'Who else? They didn't get their way this evening so they took it out on me.'

'Have you seen him?'

'His lights are out and his door's locked. It might not actually have been him but it's a pound to a penny it's his crowd. Suppose I should be grateful it was only stones. Could have been petrol bombs.' He picked up one of the small rocks normally used as a border for the rose garden. 'But these are bad enough. What if it had hit me on the topper when I was in bed? That could have been it. Curtains for Hansford.'

Robert nodded. Hansford had no need of a more responsive audience. He put his hands on his hips, pushing back the pockets of his pinstripe jacket. 'I must say, though, you and Chetwynd made a pretty good spectacle. Just about brought the house down. I didn't get what he was on about, but Jan Simpson didn't seem to like it so it must have been basically okay. Actually, anything would have been okay after her appalling drivel. Did you plan it?'

'No. Nor did he.'

'Queer cove.'

'Yes.'

Hansford described the events afterwards, which amounted to no more than chanting and mutual abuse. At least the Iraqi had been left no doubt that he wasn't welcome, though public opinion was probably of little account in his book. Thanks to Chetwynd, however, the debate was likely to make more news than it would have since it broke up in disorder and no vote had been taken. He wondered if there were a precedent. Pity most of the press had gone by then.

Robert turned to go. 'Thought any more about your shotgun?'

'Had a word with one of the lawyers about it and he said you're not allowed to shoot people even in self-defence. Said I could end up doing a turn instead of my attackers. No wonder the bloody country's going to the dogs.'

'Appalling.'

'I'm getting a baseball bat.'

'Better than nothing.'

'I'll see the Bursar in the morning about this mess — make sure I don't have to cough up for the damage myself. Could you vouch for my not being here at the time, if necessary? I mean, not provoking it. I know you can't really but you know what I mean.'

Robert yawned. 'Yes, fine.'

'Thanks. It's good to know one has friends.' Hansford stared with embarrassing sincerity. 'Want a drink? At least they didn't smash that.'

'Another time, thanks. I'm knackered.'

'Did you see your bike?'

He had forgotten again. 'No, where?'

'I put in the racks by the lodge. Couldn't see anything wrong. Nothing pinched.'

'Probably because there's nothing left on it to pinch. Thanks very much, though.'

'That wouldn't stop some of them these days. They just pinch things because they're not theirs. Sure you won't have a quick sniffle? I can't offer a selection like Tim but I nicked some of the old man's brandy last vac.'

Robert accepted because he was embarrassed at having forgotten the bike. They made a rough clearance of the mess and sat. Hansford talked about the international situation and Schools, the latter subject providing Robert with the impetus to leave. Leave-taking was prolonged, however, by further discussion of Hansford's personal security. Robert again described the escape route up to the next floor although, as he later pointed out, he had never done it himself and being anxious to go he may have exaggerated its ease.

A light came from under the door of his room. When he opened it he saw Gina sitting by the window, reading his copy of James Hogg's *The True Memoirs and Confessions of a Justified Sinner*. She had brushed her hair and changed into a long dark skirt, a white blouse and a wide black belt with gold buttons.

He remained by the door. She smiled but did not put down the book. 'I was thinking you must be with some lady love.'

'I might have been bringing her back.'

'I thought of that, too, but assumed she'd prefer her own room to yours. It's so cheerless, like a barracks. Why do you live like this?'

'I've got used to it. I don't notice.'

'Of course you notice. You're just a poser.'

'Well.' He shrugged and sat on the floor with his back against the wall.

She laughed. 'There, look at you now, ignoring the chair. If you really didn't notice you wouldn't bother to do that. You'd sit on it because it's the easy and obvious thing to do.'

'But I like sitting like this.'

'Back to the wall?'

He asked what she thought of the book and then started talking rapidly about sin.

She soon looked bored. 'Are you going to let Malcolm back or do De Flores yourself?'

'Is that why you came?'

'Malcolm's getting worse as he gets more frightened. You're better.'

'But I'm not an actor. I'm not really any good.'

'You don't need to be. You just need to be adequate. You are that.'

'Thanks.' Taking over Malcolm's part would mean a great deal of extra work. Acting opposite Gina would be a challenge, of course, but he felt he had challenge enough already and did not seek more. 'I'm not sure about directing and taking on De Flores. Not sure I've got the time and energy.'

'Modesty ill-becomes you.' She put down the book, uncrossed her legs and came over to him. She reached for his hand and wrapped her fingers round one of his. 'Come on.'

She led him into the bedroom where the light from the main room came through the half-open door. He leaned against the wall whilst she undressed and neither helped nor resisted when she undressed him. He felt detached and calm but his heart beat treacherously fast. She embraced him and they half stumbled on to the bed.

Their lovemaking was ardent and repeated, impersonal, without affection. There was no sense that it was him she was making love with but there was an unexpected satisfaction in being reduced almost to anonymity. Nor did he afterwards feel the remoteness and loneliness that commonly followed coition, along with the thought that it was impossible ever to be fully honest. He felt pleasantly tired, curious about her, free for once of pretence.

'So it wasn't about Malcolm.'

'It will mean a lot of extra work for you, doing De Flores.'

'I haven't said I would.'

'You don't know the lines yet.' She pulled the sheet up over them both.

He was beginning to think about Anne again when Gina popped herself up on her elbow and pushed her hair back from her face. 'Why don't you make some coffee while I get dressed?'

'You're going?'

'You weren't going to ask me to stay, were you?'

'No.'

'Well, stop pretending.' She leaned with both forearms on his chest. 'You fool no one but yourself, you know.'

'If I do it completely it doesn't matter. I'll never know.'

'You're not that good at it.' Her hair touched his face and the full length of her body pressed warmly down upon him. He put his arms around her. For a while there was an intimacy that was lacking in their lovemaking.

'White, no sugar,' she said.

'I haven't any milk.'

130

'Find some or I shan't come again.'

When he left the bed he kissed her on the cheek. She drew sharply back. 'Why did you do that?'

'Habit, I suppose. I usually do.'

'That's what it felt like. Don't.'

There was some milk on the ledge in the washroom. When he returned she was brushing her hair. He liked the easy familiarity with which she already seemed to use his rooms, though aware that it was perhaps the transience that made it acceptable. He put on jeans, jersey and plimsoles and walked down the stairs with her. Visitors were not allowed after midnight and the lodge was shut so they headed for the unlocked back gate.

'Time was when you'd have had to climb the wall,' he said. 'It must have been more fun then.'

'If I had to climb out I'd be staying.'

'Then be thankful it's open.' He paused at the gate. 'I'll walk you home,' he added belatedly.

They talked a little about the play, then walked in companionable silence. At her doorstep he was about to kiss her goodnight when she stepped back.

'Tomorrow at seven?'

'What?'

'The rehearsal.'

'Oh, yes, yes. Seven.'

She smiled. 'Goodnight, De Flores.'

It was still warm and he enjoyed the walk back. The rough texture of the jersey on his skin made him feel carefree and vigorous. Not even the perfunctory cheep of a bird sounding the knell on another night's sleep could dispel his euphoria. He ran up the stairs three at a time.

Unless he overslept Robert regularly had breakfast in hall. He liked the routine and it was never crowded. Only alternative places were laid, and no one spoke. People ate slowly and poured tea from a two-gallon pot. On the way he would pick up his copy of *The Times* from the lodge. He read very little of it but his pleasure was in finding it

131

in the lodge each day with his name written in blue biro. He couldn't afford the paper, and often talked of stopping it.

The news was again of the latest developments in the Middle East. Reporting them must have become difficult by then, partly because everyone was waiting and nothing was happening and partly because, despite the danger and urgency, the story had run for over a month and was boring. The Soviet ambassador had been summoned to the White House and there was speculation about a meeting between the Soviet and American leaders. At home a Government spokesman denied rumours of petrol rationing. At the same time the Department of Transport asked motorists not to keep their tanks topped up since this would create an unnecessary shortage in advance of a possible real one. Tim had already spoken of topping up. The thought of doing so reminded Robert that the Jaguar was back in the dons' car park and he still hadn't found anywhere else to put it.

At the bottom of the wide wooden staircase leading out of hall he saw Chetwynd standing like a carving, one arm folded across his stomach and the other pressed against his cheek. He looked tired and drawn and showed no recognition until Robert was level with him.

'A word with you, please.'

They fell in step around the quad but Chetwynd said nothing until they reached the soft turf of the Fellows' Garden.

'Thank you for what you did in the shop, and the Union.'

'Thank you for the painting. Tim's kept it in his room but I'll get it back sometime. Maybe you'll save me from something one day.'

'Such self-effacement is never honest. You nearly always have breakfast, don't you? At least it's better here than in most colleges. I've eaten in nearly all. No one notices. They don't realize the meal tokens are different.

I take precautions, of course. There's usually a list of people who live out in each lodge and I select a name in advance. The only problem is women.' They paused beneath the copper beech. 'At breakfast, I mean. They ruin it by talking. They have to, it's a compulsion, like dogs peeing. It doesn't matter what about, if they see each other they have to speak. I avoid the mixed colleges.'

'Not so easy now.'

'No. So please thank God, if your studies ever puts you in touch, for sparing this one. Though I'm told there are elements in the SCR anxious to fall in with the fad. The Chaplain is against it, of course. Quite properly. One needs a refuge. The President is torn between his natural horror of the sex and his desire to appear liberal. Not even the women's colleges are for it. No one actually wants it. It's simply fashion.'

They stood looking back across the garden. The sky was again monotonously blue and the morning sun sparkled in the famous stained-glass windows of the chapel. A gardener watered roses. From not far away came the sound of traffic, acceptably muffled by the intervening walls.

Chetwynd nodded towards the chapel. 'That's what I want to talk about. Rather, what's beneath it. The crypt. With your help I want to move in this morning.'

'You're going to live in it?'

'It's the noise in the New Building. If I stay a night longer I shall take an axe to every sound system and hi-fi in the place. Not that the college authorities would seriously object but the destructive urge, once indulged, is insatiable. I'd start on the furniture, move on to the people, then the buildings and finally myself — a grand finale, running round like a decapitated chicken, spouting blood and swiping at everything. But I don't want it yet.'

'Better move into the crypt, then.'

'Easier, that's all. I often run away from temptations. That's why I gave you the revolver and the bullet.'

'We've still got them.'

'I hope you have. And don't do anything silly. I shall probably want them back.' They headed for the New Building. 'I'll leave some things in my room to make it look occupied but the important stuff I'll take.'

It was not difficult to move him since he did not have much, though what there was was tidy and cared for. Many of the books had clearly been stolen.

'This,' said Chetwynd, holding a large illustrated history of the piano, 'was Blackwell's pride and joy. The display copy, especially mounted and guarded. Five days of planning. My greatest achievement. I steal mainly from Blackwell's because I hate them. They're so pleased with themselves and so hot on shoplifters. I steal from other shops only if they offend me. Libraries I never touch, a despicable crime. If only the Bodleian would appoint me as custodian I would reduce their losses dramatically. I can always tell a thief.'

He explained that he had discovered a way into the crypt via a lavatory under the stairs adjoining the chapel. The wall opposite the toilet had a door which looked like a cupboard but actually opened on to stone steps.

'What happens if someone's in the loo when you want to come in or out?' asked Robert.

'When I'm in I'll lock the lavatory door from the inside. Those in need will find another. If someone's using it while I'm out I'll wait for him or her to finish. I shall only ever been seen entering or leaving the loo. Perfect explanation. Also, when I'm in I shall have the loo to myself, something I've always cherished. Nothing like a leisurely evacuation. One of the greatest physical pleasures.'

'I wish I had one to myself.'

'You can use this if you give me sufficient notice.'

'I'm not sure I'm that regular. It depends what I eat.'

'Train yourself. I do. I have the main one at 10.30 and sometimes a subsidiary at 6.45.'

Robert smiled. 'Being with you makes me feel quite normal.'

'It's not being with me. I suspect you always feel normal to yourself. I never do, you see, which is why I talk, talk, talk but rarely act. I fear to act. You, on the other hand, are capable of acting. Everything feels normal to you because it's you that's doing it — yes?'

'Too early. Ask later.'

The crypt was used as a lumber room for old college furniture discarded in favour of newer, less comfortable fittings. They cleared a space in a corner and positioned camp-bed, desk and chair. The space was invisible from the main entrance, which was in any case practically never used. A 60–watt bulb gave enough light for reading.

'If I'm absent on the morning of my first paper,' Chetwynd said, 'you will know where to find the body. But don't tell anyone. Leave it so that future generations may find a skeleton bent over *Beowulf*. On the nights before Schools my ghost will wail through every quadraphonic in the New Building.'

'You're mad.'

'This keeps me sane. Look to yourself.'

Robert left Chetwynd to settle in and went to Tim's room. Tim was sitting at his desk, wearing only a small white towel. His body was very thin and white, his expression distant and abstracted. The curtains were drawn as usual and the room was lit only by the brass lamp.

'You working?' asked Robert, surprised.

'Wondering why I don't. Been sitting here all night.'

Robert started to withdraw. 'Okay. See you.'

'Don't go.' Tim got up and began slowly assembling his coffee apparatus. 'And I won't work today because I sat up all night. And I won't work this evening because we've got that supper at Dr Barry's.' He emptied the water out of the window, looking down afterwards to see if anyone was beneath.

Robert realized with a start that he had forgotten about

the supper arranged weeks earlier as one of a series for Schools candidates. He could not imagine how he could have let it slip his mind. 'Chetwynd's moved into the crypt because of the noise in the New Building. Don't blame him. I'd hate it, wouldn't you?'

'What?'

'The noise. Hate it.'

'Suppose so.'

Tim was still withdrawn and lethargic. His movements were mechanical, his eyes dull and hopeless.

'Something worrying you?' Robert asked, expecting to hear about Suzanne.

Tim smiled thinly. 'Nothing worries me.' He smiled again, more humorously. 'That's what been worrying me all night. Once I get talking I stop worrying.'

Eventually the college bell rang for midday. Tim opened the curtains a few inches. 'If you've got no striptease with Gina lined up come out to a pub in the country. Another pub. No companions this time. I want to fill up with petrol on the way back.'

'I must learn some lines before rehearsal.'

'Was that the work you said you were going to do?'

'Yes.'

'Bring them with you.'

They headed north until turning off the main road towards Great Tew, a thatched village in decay. The land-lord had lived in a large house hidden by trees. He could not afford to maintain the village but refused to sell houses to weekenders or to people unconnected with it. Unable to afford to repair or to buy, many of the tenants had moved away and their homes had fallen into ruin. Some remained and prospered, others just got by. A few cottages were in good condition with trim thatch, repointed brickwork and well-stocked gardens. Others such as the pub were intact in the front but collapsing at the back. Many more were derelict, with cracked and bulging walls and collapsed roofs. Chicken scratched amongst damp broken floorboards, the gardens were

136

hopelessly overgrown, wells and rusty water pumps lurked in the grass. The village stocks were dilapitated but complete. The impression was of a place visited by plague or famine.

Conversation in the bar, murmured and softly accented, stopped when they entered. The villagers were wary of newsmen, council officials and do-gooders. Talk resumed when Robert and Tim took their cheese rolls and Guinnesses to the window.

Afterwards they followed a track past a ruined smithy, then took a footpath across the field at the back. They passed well-stocked flowering gardens better preserved than their cottages and were followed for a part of the way by a black bantam. Robert, picking up a stick to throw, accidentally frightened it. At the bottom of the field a few fly-pestered cattle were tucked into the hedge. They gazed mournfully, their tails twitching. Robert took off his shirt. His shoulders were red from doing the same when punting.

'One day soon we'll wake up and there'll be a Schools paper,' said Tim. 'What then?'

'It'll be too late to worry.'

'It's the bit before it's too late that worries me.'

'Something worries you then.'

'I don't believe they're all-important but I can't convince myself they're utterly trivial. And I hate anything in-between.'

Robert threw his stick into the hedge. ' "Because thou art lukewarm and neither cold nor hot, I will spew thee out of my mouth." '

Beyond the hedge was a house so tumbled down it was hard to distinguish it from the overgrown bank. Brambles merged with the roof, grass grew in the gutters, weeds through the walls. Robert sat on the kitchen step and went through his lines. Tim prompted from within, sitting on the floor against the old black kitchen range. Bits of plaster had fallen from the ceiling and as Tim read he rubbed them into the floorboards with the palm of his hand. After a while Robert put his copy down and recited the lines with his head in his hands. The sun slanted across the doorstep on to his bare back. During one unusually long pause, when Tim was about to prompt, Robert spoke without looking round. 'Have you ever lost sleep over anyone?'

Tim stopped moving his hand amongst the plaster. 'No.'

'Eaten less food?'

'No.'

'Ever met anyone you thought you couldn't live without?'

'No.'

'Do you think you could feel that strongly about anyone?'

'I don't know.'

'Which means no.'

Tim picked up a handful of plaster and threw it over Robert's head and shoulders. Some stuck in his hair. 'Suzanne still has a teddy bear. I feel quite strongly about that.'

They followed a track past a farm and back to the village. There was a butcher open three mornings a week and a general store and post office. Through the store's small window they could see sweets, bicycle pumps, wool, batteries, paraffin, bacon, hairclips and packets of Rizla Greens. Tim bought a local paper. He was served by an old lady with whom he exchanged appropriate remarks about the weather while stroking the fluffy cat that was sitting on a box of chocolates. In the back room an old man slept in an armchair by an open stove.

'What did you do that for?' asked Robert when he came out.

'Nothing. I just like going into those places.'

They filled up with petrol on the ring road. By the time they got back the afternoon was almost over. Tim walked along to the covered market. It was shutting when he got there, filled with the noise and bustle of people going home. He lingered by the shoe shop in the Turl, wondering about leather boots. Robert went for his run.

Chapter Eight

The supper with Anne and Dr Barry was early, partly so that Anne should not be late to bed and partly to accommodate Robert's having to go to rehearsal. Tim forecast that it would be like a condemned man's last meal, though Schools were still over a week away.

He lay long in his bath and dressed slowly afterwards, savouring the solitude. When Robert arrived, apparently brisk and cheerful, he adapted to what he thought Robert in cheerful mood would want. It was a process requiring neither consciousness nor effort, but it made him aware of the inevitable falsehood in any of his dealings with others.

'This may turn out to be better than we thought,' Robert said. 'I found out who the other guests are — Hansford and Orpwood. Could end up with blood on the carpet.'

'And rival petitions circulating the table.'

Robert did not look forward to seeing Dr Barry. He had told no one about the Bursar's secretary but the thought continued to make him sad, not simply on Anne's behalf but generally. Nor had he told Tim that he had seen Suzanne at the Union with David Long. He felt a growing sense of hopelessness, which was why he had made himself breezily purposeful.

When they arrived they found the lodgers out and Anne upstairs. Dr Barry, looking harrassed, was carrying chairs through the dining-room windows to the lawn. His manner was as breezy as Robert's.

'Her idea, ten minutes ago,' he said. 'Everything neatly set up in the house, easy, comfortable, no logistical prob-

140

lems, and suddenly it has to be on the lawn. Has to be —
the weather may break soon, the last chance this summer,
more difficult to eat out when the baby comes, you lot
will prefer it and God knows what else.' He lowered his
voice and stood very close, a habit he had that made
nearly everyone uncomfortable. 'One of the spin-offs of
the interesting condition. Great importance attaches to
trivia, other things pass them by altogether. Same with
sex. One moment you're accused of being unloving and
ignoring them and the next they're begging to be left
alone. No that there's much sex in marriage, anyway. You
wait and see.'

Hansford arrived wearing a blazer and school tie,
Orpwood a bright blue tie and tweed jacket in which he
looked uncomfortable. His shirt collar was considerably
larger than his thin neck.

Anne came slowly down the stairs, in a pink dress
that looked like a night gown. She did not glance at
her husband. 'We're eating in the garden. Hope that's
all right.'

The guests expressed appropriate pleasure. There was
a slight pause, then everyone tried to move in unison
through the dining room windows. Anne smiled at Robert
when the others had gone out, but turned away quickly
as if to forestall him. Over drinks Orpwood talked earnestly to Dr Barry about standardization of markings.

Hansford edged Robert away from the others. 'See —
he's got a blue tie on,' he said, nodding at Orpwood.
'Nearly asked him if he was defecting.' He bent to the
waist with suppressed laughter.

Next it was Orpwood who attached himself to Robert,
just as the food was being brought out. 'No idea he was
coming,' he said of Hansford. 'Do you think old Barry
did it deliberately? I mean, he can't not know.' He sipped
his white wine with nervous haste. 'This isn't bad,
though, is it? I don't often have wine, usually beer. Not
that I've anything against it. If it's wet I'll drink it. How
about you?'

Robert's glass was already empty. He had noticed several times recently that he was the first to finish. 'Same with me, I suppose, except that it varies a bit depending on where I am and who I'm with.'

'That's because drinking's a social convention. Nothing to do with thirst.' Tim and Hansford were helping bring out plates and food. Orpwood watched warily. 'Do you think we ought to give a hand?'

'No need at the moment. We can help clear up.'

Orpwood looked relieved. 'Good idea. Don't let me forget.'

He drew closer, his back to the others. 'Someone told me they've got girl lodgers here.'

Robert was careful not to smile. 'I suspect they're out tonight. I don't think we're missing much.'

Orpwood nodded knowledgably. 'Very likely not.'

They sat at a garden table and ate rice, salad and luke-warm meat. It had never occured to Robert that Anne might not be a good cook. He had never thought of her as having to do anything like that. Nor, he realized as he munched a tasteless piece of lettuce, had he ever thought of her as a person who ate and digested like other people, a person in whose stomach were acids and foul juices, whose kidneys, bladder and long intestine functioned unceasingly and were warm and stinking. She ate heartily, laughing and talking, her brown eyes shining. He hated what he was thinking but would not let go of it, and wilfully imagined the gastric slime.

Conversation moved from the role of ceremony in public life to the importance of gesture, public or private. It was becoming rather like a tutorial. Hansford and Orpwood, subdued by convention, competed in labyrin-thine reasonableness without once addressing each other directly. Tim made occasional forays, once or twice catching Robert's eyes and not quite suppressing a smile. Anne argued earnestly and with unusual abruptness. Robert thought of cancer cells, silently mutating. It was like thinking something forbidden. There could be no

142

hope, no change but for the worse, nothing would last. He looked up into the branches of a poplar. Its leaves shimmered and trembled against the limitless evening sky.

As in the tutorial, it was Dr Barry who recalled him. 'What do you think, Robert?'

'About what?'

Everyone laughed except Tim, who smiled slightly.

'Jan Palach, or rather his self-immolation during the Prague Spring in 1968 when the Russians marched in. Are such gestures useful, futile, virtuous, foolish, brave?'

'Futile,' interrupted Anne firmly.

'In that case only, or at all times and in all places?'

'Always. You don't help anything by doing away with yourself. It's much better to try to do something about whatever it is.' She spoke doggedly with her head down, addressing her empty plate. 'Or you just have to put up with it and try to do good in some other way.'

'I agree,' said Hansford, holding up his hand as if defending her. 'Unless you can see your death will help in some way — no greater love than this and all that — it's a waste of time. I must say I don't fancy it myself very much, not the way he did it, anyway.'

'That's not really agreeing,' said Anne quietly.

Dr Barry ignored her and looked at Orpwood, whose words tumbled out. 'Well, no, but I mean I basically agree with the proposition that the gesture is futile unless it leads to a concrete result which I can't see happening in the kind of case we're talking about. And if it did it wouldn't be a gesture, it would be — you know — a means to an end.'

Dr Barry folded his arms. 'How interesting. This is clearly a more pragmatic student generation than Jan Palach's. Or perhaps just British.'

'No, I don't mean I approve or disapprove in principle,' continued Orpwood. 'Just that I don't see the point of it — unless there is a point.'

'Quite,' said Hansford firmly.

'Robert's a pragmatist, I imagine?' asked Dr Barry.

Robert shrugged and smiled. 'Well, I could see that someone might do it for the hell of it.'

'But people don't do that,' said Anne quickly. 'And I don't think you believe they do. It's completely negative. No one lives like that.'

'Perhaps they never get round to doing anything about it.'

Dr Barry laughed. 'Too apathetic to be negative? Pleasing thought.' His eyes twinkled. 'Tim agrees, I bet.'

Tim tried to turn it away with a facetious remark about the oil crisis and the waste of petrol. They laughed awkwardly except for Anne, who continued to stare at Robert. Her brown eyes looked hard and brimful.

'But what do you really think?' she asked.

Robert smiled again, feeling increasingly uncomfortable. He did not want to be drawn in. He had no strong views, was aware only of an absence of feeling. 'Well, if you want to do it, why not? Assuming whoever it was was responsible only for himself.'

'Don't be ridiculous, you don't really think that. We're all responsible for each other.' She continued to stare, then added slowly, 'I don't believe that's what you really think.'

'At least Jan Palach died for something, which is more than the rest of us will do. We'll just die. A bit later, that's all.'

'And the fact that we're still talking about him shows he achieved something,' said Dr Barry.

Anne still stared. Her eyes had softened and were almost pleading but she said no more. Robert stared evenly back. For a moment he was pleased at having provoked, perhaps even hurt, but when he thought of the Bursar's secretary again he shook his head very slightly, as if to indicate he hadn't been serious. Anne smiled and looked down.

Tim was the first to go, dishonestly pleading work. While saying goodbye he seemed suddenly to become conscious of leaving with unseemly haste and so became uncharacteristically formal and protracted in his thanks. Hansford and Orpwood stayed for a short while, then left together, pausing with cumbersome politeness at the gate. Despite his rehearsal, Robert accepted Anne's invitation to help with the washing-up. Dr Barry went upstairs to make some telephone calls.

'Wash or dry?' she asked.

'Don't mind.'

'You should mind more.' She threw him his tea towel. 'This negativity won't do. You should get married.'

'Me?'

She laughed at his expression. 'Marriage is so relaxing. That's what's nice about it. Unforced intimacy. It stops you from sinking in on yourself. You grow into it. It expands you.' She laughed again and put her hand on her stomach. 'That wasn't deliberate, I promise.'

'I'll bear it in mind.'

'David and me, we're very close, you know. It's very sustaining. People talk about regrets but I really haven't any. We're very, very fond of each other.' Her eyes shone now with sincerity and she talked urgently, as if advertising something. 'It must show, doesn't it?'

He took a dripping plate from her. 'You look very well on it.'

Dr Barry came noisily downstairs, complaining about people who were never there when you wanted them. Robert said he had to go.

'On with rehearsing?' asked Dr Barry cheerfully. 'I always imagine you as nocturnal. I suppose you do your work at night?'

Robert hesitated. 'I am pretty nocturnal, yes.'

On the doorstep Anne slipped her arm around Dr Barry's waist. He put his round her shoulders.

'I've been trying to persuade Robert to get married,' she said.

'You should, you should,' said Dr Barry. 'Do you good. It's a good institution. Does everyone good.'

Robert nodded and smiled as he backed away down the garden path. 'Thanks for dinner.'

The next day was Founder's Day, which the college celebrated with a free feast in the evening. It was said that at one time swans were eaten but during recent years it had become traditional to have an unseasonal Christmas dinner, with summer pudding substituted for Christmas pudding. Before the meal there was a service in chapel at which the President preached the Founder's sermon. This could be about anything the President chose and differed from other sermons preached by himself or the Chaplain only in that it was published in the college gazette. Those reading theology were expected, though not compelled, to attend.

For over a year now Robert had avoided his fellow theologians. He had nothing against them. Pale, polite, earnest young men, they almost all were destined for the Church, and mostly High Church at that — evangelism did not flourish alongside the academic study of biblical texts. Robert avoided them because he felt fraudulent in their company, and decided to attend the service because he felt guilty about avoiding them. He had been at rehearsal most of the day and there was more later that night so the evening was written off anyway.

'I'll come with you,' said Tim.

'What for?'

Tim was momentarily awkward. 'Well — to see what it's like.'

Robert usually forgot Tim's intermittent interest in religion. Most of the time Tim was unconcernedly agnostic but occasionally a potential for religious enthusiasm showed itself. He would make half-appreciative, half-mocking remarks, quoting Nietzsche and Pascal and sometimes the Bible — not, Robert discovered

146

one day, from his reading but from the *Oxford Dictionary of Quotations*.

They arrived, late and gowned, to find the President already launched upon his sermon. They tried to slip in quietly to a pew about half way down but Tim banged his foot on the back of the one in front, causing the President to falter and a few of the small congregation to turn around. Robert looked down as if in prayer, hiding his smile and thinking of Chetwynd, the God-hater, working his malign influence from below.

The President continued with one hand on the lectern, the other hidden in the fold of his surplice.

' . . . which brings me back full circle to Traherne; "We love we know not what and therefore everything allures us." Traherne saw love as a reaching out from oneself. For the Christian this is ultimately a reaching-out for God. We reach but what do we find? The experience of God is rarely direct — remember, "No man has seen God at any time; the only begotten Son which is in the bosom of the Father, He hath declared Him."

'For most of us the experience of God is filtered through the world. Our reaching out is a blind response to His presence. We strive towards Him, we yearn for Him, often without knowing it. In loving what is of limited value we learn to love what is of value without limit. As we progress our love has less to do with particulars, more with love itself, which is God. This journey has no end but itself. It has to be made, not to take us anywhere but that we may discover the end within.

'But this happens only when we fully love, not when we egotistically grab things, hug them to ourselves, make of everything a passion. That is why our love for each other so often fails. In such cases it is not the other person we love but an image of our own making. When a person fails the image, or breaks out of it, everything fails. And this because we loved not them at all but ourselves. Them, we hardly knew.

'It is only in loving that we discover what there is to

147

love. Really to love is very hard. It begins with an acceptance of your own vulnerability and ends with renunciation of yourself. It has to be fought for every minute of
every day. It means rediscovering your essential self, that
self from which, without God, you have become
estranged. Hardened by habit and selfishness, rediscovering our deeper selves brings both joy and pain. It
may be a sudden birth or slow but it is never easy. So it
is with God. He dwells in a secret room within us and
our real journeys are inwards. But we make them by
reaching out, by being generous and vulnerable. The goal
of love is itself — God — and we cannot reach Him
without renunciation. We must in life be prepared to lose
everything that we value, all that makes it worthwhile,
every person, everything. For assuredly we shall,
prepared or not.

'Remember Christ on the cross. Did He not then make
plain once and for all the nature of God — ultimate self-
giving? And was He not, even He, at the end deprived —
"My God, my God, why hast thou forsaken me?" God
left Him. Think of that.

'The meaning of this is that we must give all to gain
all. There is no middle way. Failure to love is the real
death, it is to lose all without hope. Most of us sense this
but normally we love only in part, as we live only in part.
To paraphrase Traherne, "We know not how to love and
therefore everything eludes us." '

The President stepped heavily down from the pulpit.
A hymn was sung, the Chaplain said a short prayer for
world peace and the service ended.

Outside the President and Chaplain talked together in
a corner of the quad. They parted abruptly, each with his
cassock billowing.

There was still time before dinner. Tim proposed they
walk in the Fellows Garden. 'That was something,' he
said.

'What?'

'The sermon.'

148

'Oh, yes.'

They walked slowly, heads bowed, hands behind backs, feet crunching the gravel. 'Now I feel like a don,' said Tim.

Robert was lost in his own thoughts. Tim trod with slow care as if he were brimful and trying not to spill something. 'So, we have only to love,' he added.

'That's all.'

'Is it true, do you think?'

'Maybe.'

'But you don't care?'

Robert gazed at the roses without noticing them. 'I used to.'

A window opened and the Chaplain leaned out. He had removed his surplice and his white shirt was open at the neck, strikingly setting off his fine quick features and blonde hair.

'Come and have a drink before dinner,' he said.

The Chaplain's room was lined from floor to ceiling with books. Two of the chairs, a trunk and a small table were Far Eastern exotica.

'Tim liked the sermon,' said Robert bluntly.

The Chaplain poured sherry into glasses of a kind given away with petrol. 'It's the first time you've been to chapel, isn't it? This is dry, is that all right? Yes, it was quintessentially presidential. It's always either love or redemption. He takes turn and turn about. Your health.'

They sat and there was a pause until Tim spoke with unusual energy. 'I was struck by the way he tied it in with "My God, my God, why hast thou forsaken me?" I'd never thought of it like that.'

'Dear old Psalm 22; "Why art thou so far from helping me, from the words of my groaning?" I say that every time I mark Schools papers.'

'Psalm 22?'

The Chaplain's eyes shone as if with drink, excessive good humour or malice. 'Jesus quotes the psalms throughout the crucifixion. I'm surprised Robert hasn't told you — unless he's forgotten all of his NT study? Each of the four accounts of the crucifixion shows Jesus quoting from the Old. Correct, Robert?'

Robert nodded.

'In fact, Psalm 22 was the model for the crucifixion — "They have pierced my hands and feet — I can count all my bones — they stand and gloat over me; they divide my garments among them and for my rainment they cast lots." It was most likely propaganda by the evangelists trying to prove Jesus's continuity with the Old Testament. That was the main concern of the early Christians. They were fighting for the inheritance of orthodox Judaism. They wanted to remain Jews. But they lost and were called Christians instead. Hence two religions with the same text.'

'I didn't know that.'

The Chaplain's eyes were softer but still smiling. 'Hope I haven't dampened your ardour.'

'No, no. It's very interesting.'

'Of course, it's possible that Jesus did say some of what's attributed to him. He probably knew his Old Testament pretty well so he could have quoted from it if he was feeling talkative, though the fact that he makes different remarks in each of the four gospels is a bit awkward; and where they are similar it's usually because they've taken it from Mark or used a common source unknown to us.'

'So what really happened?'

'No one knows. All we can say is that something happened. Something very out of the ordinary to have provoked such fuss. Many other things happened. There were other messiahs, other prophets — but none had an effect like this. That's really all we can say. Though there was Paul, of course. There wouldn't have been a Church without him.' The college bell rang for dinner. 'Anyway, you must tell the President you liked his sermon. He was bemoaning falling attendance last week but if you praise him for today I might be able to persuade him to stand in for me next Sunday.'

'I'll mention it.'

The Chaplain finished his own sherry. 'Schools will be on you both very soon, won't they? When do they start?' The question was addressed to Tim.

'The seventeenth. No, there's one paper on the afternoon of the sixteenth. The seventeenth is the first full day.'

'Are you confident?'

'About as confident as I deserve.'

Robert's sherry was untouched. The Chaplain turned in his chair. 'Robert, you look as if you're musing on failure. You've no need, I promise you.'

Robert picked up his sherry and smiled. 'Failure to love.'

'Of course.' The Chaplain smiled back. 'A very deadly sin. A real spiritual killer. The President will be pleased.'

He remarked then on the college position in the Norrington Tables, which listed colleges in order of priority according to Schools results. Norrington had been a Trinity man, and Trinity, a small, easy-going and uncompetitive college, was usually near the bottom. The Chaplain was amused by this.

The feast was a boisterous affair further enlivened by a friend of Hansford's who walked the length of the tables in order to pick up the pepper pot from someone he didn't like. He trod in summer puddings and was cheered on by the rowing club.

Afterwards Tim was to have taken some freesias to Anne to thank her for the supper but he seemed overwhelmed by lassitude, unable to make up his mind to do anything. He said he didn't want to see or speak to anyone and suggested Robert took them. Robert was keen to do so but argued quite forcibly that he should not until satisfied that Tim would not relent.

When he called he was let in by Yale Gail who said that Dr Barry was out and that Anne was in her room, reading. He found the bedroom door ajar and the light on. There was no answer to his soft knock so he cautiously stepped in.

She was in bed, lying on her side and staring at the wall through half-closed eyes, a book open on the floor. Roused by his movement she began slowly to raise herself without looking round. 'It's all right, I'm coming, I'm coming.' She moved with effort but when she saw who it was she lay down again. 'Oh, it's you.' There was a pause. 'I thought it was David.'

'I'm sorry. I thought you were awake.'

She lay as she had been, her eyes fully open but puffy. Her face looked heavier and older.

'How are you?' he asked.

'Pregnant.'

He remained by the door. 'Anything I can do? You don't look very well.'

'Not unless you want to have it for me.'

'I won't stop. I've got these for you, that's all. They're from Tim too. I'll leave them downstairs.'

She lifted her head. 'You shouldn't have. Thank you — come another day.'

'I'll come tomorrow, maybe.'

'Yes, tomorrow.'

He turned to leave but stopped as she began to sob. Her face was in the pillow and her body shook. For a few seconds he could not decide whether she would prefer him to go or stay, then he went to the bed and laid his hand on her shoulder. Gradually and laboriously she sat up and began drying her eyes on a tissue tucked in the sleeve of her nightgown. 'I hate being like this,' she whispered. 'Hate it, hate it.'

'You're sure there's nothing I can get you?' His voice sounded thicker than usual.

She blew her nose. 'Sorry. Thought you were David. Stupid of me.'

The front door opened and closed. Robert started. 'That's probably him now,' he said.

'He's been at a Philosophical Society meeting.' She

152

dabbed at her eyes again and pushed back her hair. 'They're always in the evening. I don't know why they have to be so late.'

'I'll go and see if it's him.'

'Don't go. I mean, come back when you've been.' She smiled for the first time. 'Thank you.'

Robert went noisily downstairs, as if to emphasize that he had nothing to hide. Dr Barry was in the hall. He looked surprised but smiled quickly. He took the freesias and headed for the kitchen.

'Better put them in something,' he said. 'How is she?'

'Tired.'

'It's a tiring time. Uncomfortable, too. Nothing to do but wait.' He dithered by the draining-board, then filled one of the blue and white striped mugs with water and dumped the freesias in. They were too tall and began falling out. He pushed them back twice. 'Damn.'

'Have you got a vase?' asked Robert.

'Dozens, probably. Don't ask me where, though.'

They looked around the kitchen. Robert stared without seeing. Dr Barry pointed to a glass jug on the dresser 'What about that?'

Robert fetched it. It was a heavy piece with a thick base. As he crossed the kitchen he had a sudden wilful vision of smashing Dr Barry's head with it. His head was too large for his body, anyway, and looked fragile and vulnerable. Robert imagined it flattened like the cat's head under Tim's stone. Dr Barry reached for the jug but Robert held onto it. Dr Barry's eyes were suddenly wary and nervous.

'How was your meeting?' Robert asked.

'Fine. Much as usual.' Dr Barry reached for the jug. The wariness in his eyes persisted. 'You don't approve of me, do you?'

Robert knew there had been no meeting. For a few moments he experienced a sensation of great power and clarity, but he shrank from indulging it. 'It's up to you what you do.'

He let Dr Barry take the jug. Dr Barry's eyes had lost

153

their wariness but retained a quick nervous perception. 'It takes marriage to face you with your faults,' he said. 'Before that they're simply characteristics. I believe St Paul said something similar about sin and the law, but you'd know all about that.' He smiled tentatively. 'I hope I can rely on your discretion.'

Robert thought of the doubt about the baby. He nodded and said nothing.

Dr Barry put the freesias in the jug. 'There, that's perfect. I'll leave them on the table here. Whatever she thinks about gesture, Anne's a woman where flowers are concerned. She'll love you for them.'

'Tim got them. They're his.'

Dr Barry laughed. 'So much for gesture. Cock-eyed as everything else.'

Chapter Nine

All the college boats improved their positions during Eights Week. The first eight bumped Keble to become Head of the River. Dinner in hall was noisy and prolonged, with much sconcing. The captain of rowing was carried to the JCR bar where celebrations continued into the early hours. Damage was paid for by the rowing club, which had also to pay for that caused in Keble during a midnight raid. A chemist who had never been known to drink was found unconscious in the quad.

The official celebrations were two nights later. Quieter members of college who could spent the night away. Everyone said it was hard on those with Schools approaching but it was pointed out that some of the rowers were also in that position. Although it was no longer possible to get a fourth class degree, the belief that it would have been honourable persisted in some quarters.

Robert's rehearsal started late that night. He had meant to work beforehand but instead spent the time trying to alter the blocking in the final act. But he wasn't concentrating and what he did was really only tinkering. Eventually, unwilling any longer to endure their silent reproach, he decided to take his unopened books back to the college library. It was not locked until midnight and once, during his first year when he worked hard, he had studied until 11.30 and had then lain down by the *Procedings of the Aristotelian Society*. He had had to wait until morning to be let out by the porter.

The library and the wide wooden stairs leading to it

were deserted when he went in. He lingered over books he was supposed to have read long ago, books that the Chaplain now said might be worth a final glance, until the shouting in the quad, distant at first, grew alarmingly closer. He went quickly to the door. The shouting was already at the bottom of the stairs, but out of sight, round the corner. It was obviously the rowing club, intent perhaps on sacking the library. He had started down when the shouting was drowned by the sudden revving of an engine, deafening in the confined space. There was a crash which shook the stairs, followed by laughing and swearing and shouting. He hesitated, then continued down.

Rounding the corner he saw a red-haired man whose name he did not know on a motorbike which pointed up to the stairs. Man and bike were held upright by a dozen or so dinner-jacketed and dishevelled companions. He knew most of them and they roared a mixture of challenge and greeting. The man on the bike grinned. He kick-started it and let out the clutch.

There was another concussing noise. The bike leapt a couple of steps then reared up like a horse, stalled and toppled sideways. The rider fell amongst his supporters and the bike crashed against the wall and lay still, the front wheel pointing upwards and spinning by itself. The shouting and guffawing began again.

No one remarked on Robert's attitude at the time but several remembered it later. He made no effort to get out of the way but stood, one hand in his trouser pocket and the other hanging limply at his side, as the bike leapt towards him. It fell short but he couldn't have known it would. He was unflinching. Only after the bike had fallen did he move to the side of the stairs and try to slip past the scrum. It was then that Hansford saw him.

Hansford bellowed across the few feet that separated them. His bow tie was missing, his shirt unbuttoned to the waist and one of his jacket pockets torn. His hair fell

156

straight forward on to his face and his mouth gaped open. 'Robert!' he shouted again. 'Give us a hand!'

Robert stepped round the bike and Hansford clapped him heavily on the shoulder. 'Good you're here. Bloody good.'

'Nice to be here.'

'Chap's trying to get the bike upstairs.'

Robert saw it was an elderly Enfield. 'Pity to spoil that. They're rare.'

'Won't spoil it. Going to put it in the library. Give us a hand.'

'I'm not sure there's much I can do.'

'Bunch of idiots tonight. All pissed. Can't get anything right.'

The rider remounted to the accompaniment of shouted instructions. Hansford leaned confidentially towards Robert, breathing alcohol. 'This is not the end of it tonight. Going to do more.'

'What?'

'Orpwood look out.' He added something else which was lost in the roar of the engine and then fell to, pushing on the back of the saddle before the rider was ready to go.

Robert left unnoticed and was soon out of sight. The engine revved furiously for a few seconds, there was another crash and then more shouting.

Much later, after rehearsal that night he walked back to college with Gina. He knew the others in the cast would notice but no longer minded.

'Do you have any aims?' she asked after a while.

'What?'

'Anything you want to achieve. Aims for life.'

'Finishing the play.'

'No job?'

'Haven't thought about it.'

'It's too late, even if you did. Schools? Do you want a first?'

'Too late, even if I could.'

'No aims at all, then?'

157

'Afraid not. Is that disgraceful?'

She smiled. 'It's one thing I like about you. It's different from everyone else here. Most people are ambitious. Except, the odd thing is, you're not that different. You're the sort of person that normally has aims, much more than most people. And you enjoy being ruthless, as you did with Malcolm.'

'Do I?'

'Don't say you didn't. It thrilled you. But it's hard to imagine you without an aim. I don't know what will become of you; you won't just do nothing.'

'I'll keep you informed.'

'That won't be easy. I'm going to Italy for the summer.'

He almost said he would go with her, though he had no money, but the moment passed.

Books and papers littered his staircase. Turning the corner, they came upon records, cassettes, clothes and a broken lampshade. They had to climb over a mattress. On the landing outside Orpwood's room they found the bedframe.

Orpwood stood just inside the door, his dark eyes bulging and dazed. 'It's those rowing bastards,' he said flatly. 'Hansford and his lot. I've only just got back but I know it must have been them. It's probably revenge for Hansford's windows, but I didn't do that. I know who did, but it wasn't me and I didn't put them up to it. If they've broken my stereo I shall bloody — ' he trailed off, sounding near to tears.

'We'll give you a hand to clear up,' said Robert.

'No, I can do it, thanks.'

'It won't take long with three of us,' said Gina.

Orpwood relented and became less apathetic the more they did. He cast surreptitious glances at Gina and by the time his room was restored to something like order he was aggressively cheerful.

'Hansford and his crowd will pay for this. You have to play them at their own game sometimes. But it's basically a political struggle and this is just the beginning.' The

158

thought obviously pleased him. 'Yes, it's all got to be seen in a politicial perspective. Do you want coffee?'

Robert hesitated. 'No, thanks, we're — we're going upstairs.' Gina was starting to laugh. 'Give us a shout if you need any help in the night,' Robert added with forced carelessness to cover his own further embarrassment.

Orpwood smiled. 'Thanks. Cheers.'

Feeling awkward made Robert desire Gina more. She paused at his door and he put his hand on her waist.

'I know now what it is you remind me of,' she said. 'A labrador.'

'Why?'

'Don't worry, it's quite endearing. Good-natured and clumsy.' She entered and sat in the armchair. 'Tell me about your former lady-love.'

'Are you jealous?'

'No, so you might as well tell me. You know you'd like to.'

'What makes you think that?'

She leaned back and lightly pushed her skirt down over her knee. 'Come on.'

'She's called Anne, and she's now married to Dr Barry and she's having a baby.'

'Was Dr Barry the reason you broke up with her?'

'Partly.'

'What's she like in bed?' Her tone was natural with no hardness or affected nonchalance.

'That's not really the point.'

'Of course it is. Everything else follows from that. You wouldn't have gone on seeing her if it was awful.'

'It's not the whole point.'

'It is for you.'

He grinned. 'You have a pretty cynical view of human nature.'

'We were talking about you.' She picked up a paper from his desk. 'What's this doing here?'

It was his application for theological college which he had left unfolded. She laughed at his discomfort.

159

'I wasn't going to send it, anyway,' he said suddenly. 'I've changed my mind.'

'Don't lie, you're hopeless when you're lying. Why do you want to do it? It sounds so unlike you. Listen.' She began reading aloud from one of his answers. 'Neglect of the Church's spiritual mission-'

He snatched the form from her, tearing it. She watched with a serious and momentarily tender expression. 'You're so silly sometimes,' she said. 'You behave more like a fool than you are.'

He shrugged and sat on the floor not far from her chair. She slipped off her shoes and raised one foot so that she could just touch him on the chin with her toe. 'Wondering what to say next?'

He took hold of her heel and squeezed it until she cried out for him to stop. He took it again, more gently. 'I think we should do it on High Table.' He had the satisfaction of seeing her look surprised.

'What on earth for?'

He didn't know. 'So I can think of it when I have dinner and see the President slurping his soup.'

She smiled indulgently. 'You were probably a very nice little boy. It's a pity. Now you're just a labrador.'

They crossed the quad furtively. From somewhere in the New Building came the sound of the rowing club carolling quieter members of the college. The tall doors of the hall were unlocked, as Robert had feared and hoped. Once inside they stood still. There was enough light to make out the long tables and benches with High Table on its raised platform at the end. The portraits were darker patches on the dark walls. It was like the chapel, which he could have suggested instead. There was the usual smell of polish and communal cooking.

'There's no chance of the rowdies bursting in on us, is there?' she asked.

'They won't come here. There's no one to wake.'

'Why are we whispering?'

'I don't know.' His normal voice was startlingly loud.

160

'Now you do,' she whispered.

They climbed on to High Table beneath the eyes of the founder.

'You should have brought some cushions.'

'It's not that hard.'

'It is.'

She twisted out from under him. 'I'll go on top.'

She hitched up her skirt. It occurred to him that the rowing club might after all burst in, intending perhaps to pile all the tables to the ceiling or lay them out for breakfast in the quad. Or the President might return in search of his pipe lighter.

It was hurriedly done and she got off with a relief that had little to do with the sexual. He lay as he was, wondering whether he would confess this to Tim or Chetwynd. A floorboard creaked.

'Come on,' she said.

They did not talk normally until outside. He felt more relieved that he would have admitted and took her hand, but she snatched it away almost immediately to light a cigarette. She threw the lighter back into her bag. 'Try doing that with someone you love.'

'You are jealous.'

'Don't be stupid.' She put her arm through his. 'It's late. Take me home.'

On his way back from her house he ran into Hansford who was walking away from college, very dishevelled, his movements abrupt and hesitant, his direction uncertain.

He stopped when he saw Robert. 'All bloody stupid really, no harm intended.' His face was heavy and sorrowful and oddly blotchy. 'Orpwood's room. Bloody mess.'

'I saw it. Postscript to your dinner?'

'Wasn't me, though. Other blokes.'

'But you put them up to it?'

'No, no. Other blokes, really. All pissed. They went

161

off. I stayed in the library. Came out for a walk. Wanted to get out.'

'I helped him clear up.'

'Good, good.' Hansford stood in bovine passivity, lumpish and crumpled.

'See you,' said Robert.

Hansford turned and walked with him. 'Me that has to watch out. They'll be after me now.'

'Assassination squads?'

'Depends on Geneva. If talks fail, political chaos, what have they got to lose? Give them what they want. No holds barred. Do anything. Should've got my gun. Keep thinking about your escape route.'

'Glad to hear it.'

The main gates were locked, and rather than walk round Robert suggested they climb the wall by the President's lodgings. It was one of his favourite spots and he had become quite adept. Hansford was not. It was amusing the first few times to watch him graze his hands and knees but it soon became wearisome. Robert suggested he went round to the back gate after all but Hansford was determined.

Eventually Robert braced himself against the wall and formed a footrest with his hands. After one or two false starts Hansford got his foot in place and heaved himself up. His knee caught Robert on the lip and made it bleed a little.

Hansford straddled the wall like a dummy. After increasingly irritated advice from Robert he lowered himself down the other side. Robert climbed with gratifying agility. The President's door was only a few feet away.

'Move back and I'll jump.'

Hansford did not move and so Robert jumped to one side of him, at which point Hansford moved. Robert tried to change direction and fell amongst the President's dustbins. There was a prolonged clanging. He lay sprawled amongst the upturned bins, blood on his lips and pains in his shin and arms. Hansford laughed.

The President's porch light came on and two windows were lit. One opened abruptly, framing the President's stocky figure. He wore a blue dressing-gown and his sparse hair stood up in tufts. Robert tried to rise, trusting his weight to the remaining upright bin, but it was empty and he pulled it over with another clang.

The President spoke crisply. 'Mr Stevens, Mr Hansford — if either of you makes any more noise tonight I shall be forced to recognize you both. Goodnight.' He closed the window firmly and the lights went out.

Hansford suppressed his laughter until they were out of earshot. 'Bloody funny,' he kept saying. 'Don't you think? Bloody funny.'

Robert wiped the blood from his mouth. His leg hurt and he limped. They crossed the dons' car park and he saw that the windscreen of the Jaguar was now all but covered with sticky labels threatening imminent removal.

'Sorry I made such a cock-up of that wall,' said Hansford, more sober now. 'Never was exactly agile. I ought to practise if I'm going to use that escape route.'

'You ought.'

'It maybe too late. They might come for me tonight.'

'I'd stay awake if I were you.'

After they parted Robert slept quickly and deeply. Some hours later, though, he woke abruptly, convinced there was someone else in his room. He lay still, eyes open, fearful, not breathing. Someone sat on the edge of his bed.

'Forgive me. It's terrible to wake anyone at any time but I am in need.'

Chetwynd's voice was low and quiet with the too precise pronunciation that indicated drunkenness. 'I have two needs. The first is conversation. I shall make no demands. I need only to know that someone is listening.'

Robert heard him go to the window where he pulled back the curtain a few inches. It was not sunrise, but a

163

pale stealthy light crept into the room. The clock on the chair ticked loudly, its hands at ten to four.

Chetwynd was wearing full subfusc, his gown properly on his shoulders, his mortarboard horizontally on his head. The tassle of his cap dangled before his left eye. He sat carefully on the edge of the bed again.

'You know this is the first day of my Schools? Of course you don't. Why should you? I'm prepared as if for ritual disembowlment — in the matter of dress, that is.'

Robert sat up. 'You been up all night?'

'I've drunk my way through to alcoholic clarity. My fear is that it might not last until I get to the examination. I write better when drunk.'

'Five and a half hours to go.'

'That's the other reason I came. No more whisky. Do you have any? I shan't drink here. I'll go back to the crypt.'

'No.' Robert never had any food or drink of his own. 'Tim has on the book shelf in his outer room. The door won't be locked.'

'I know he has but I wanted to ask and I know you better. I never take from friends. You've given the perfect reply. I shall repay him.'

Robert remembered the revolver. 'What happens if you sober up halfway through?'

'It won't matter by then. It's a question of getting myself there. What happens when I see the paper is beyond my control. I may sleep, I may doodle, I may write verse, I may write passionately about town planning in Oslo. I may even answer the question. But I know if I am not drunk I shall be unable to leave the crypt.' His teeth showed briefly in the gloom. 'Which is a fine and private place.'

Properly awake now, Robert folded his arms around his knees. 'Tim and I were thinking of trying to see you the other night.'

'As well you didn't. And you went to chapel, did you not? I saw you come out. You know my views. Neverthe-

164

less, it was a good thing to do. For you and him, not for me.' He flicked his white bow tie with one bony finger. 'This charade — it fools no one. We wear it for our own sakes, it helps us endure. The same with what you are seeking. A different kind of charade. You are in need. Understandably so. We all are. So long as you understand that in your charade the actors are also the spectators. No one else is watching. There isn't anyone, no eternal eye to see you, no everlasting ear to hear you. Except to ourselves we are without significance. And that is itself a fact without significance, even to us in the end.'

He stood outlined against the faint light of the window and ceremoniously raised his hat. 'Good day to you.'

'It's in the bookcase on the right. He won't hear you. Never hears anything.'

Chetwynd closed the bedroom door carefully and then appeared to stumble about in the other room. Robert wondered if he was looking for the pistol and bullet after all. When he heard the outer door close he got quickly out of bed and checked that the bullet was still in the pocket of his jeans. It was. He locked the outer door in case Chetwynd returned.

He got back into bed, shaking his head and smiling to himself. Much of what happened to him now seemed increasingly unreal. It was not an unpleasant state. The illusion that life was getting out of control was a comforting one. He had to get up again to close the curtains but then fell into a deep sleep in which he thought he heard, or did hear, someone knocking at the door and calling his name. He had a confused dream of Chetwynd with Hansford's voice calling and calling. He snuggled deeper into the bed.

It was one of the scouts who found Hansford the following morning. He was unconscious on the path at the back of the Old Building. An ambulance was called and he was taken away before most people were up.

The police came and two officers questioned people on

their way into breakfast. Robert found out when he went to the lodge to get his paper. It emerged that he was probably the last person to have seen Hansford. He described to the police his returning to college and Hansford's ineptitude and state of mind without at first mentioning the escape route proposal. When he did the police took it seriously and he had to show them the route, but as Hansford was found nearer his own window than Robert's or Tim's the investigation was inconclusive. The President, in whose lodgings the interviews took place, displayed a gruff perplexity.

Robert shared the general shock and made much the same remarks as most people. He suspected, though, that really he was less affected. During the police questions he found his thoughts were partly on what else he had to do that day. He could not feel sure that there really was any inward echo to the sympathy and concern he expressed. It was possible that he was no different from everyone else in this respect; possible, too, that he was unusual in being troubled by it.

He went to break the news to Tim at 11.30. Tim had just got up and was listening to his record of birdsong, a habit he still maintained despite Robert's regular scorn. Guilt about not taking Hansford seriously, about the locked door, about not feeling enough led Robert to adopt the self-righteous air of a man who had been up and about and had got to grips with the world. 'You look bloody awful, even for you.'

'So would you if you'd had someone fooling around in your room in the night. Knocked half my books off the shelf and pinched my malt.'

'That was Chetwynd. He came to me and I told him where it was. He'll pay it back. He needed it to help him get to Schools.'

Tim did not seem to mind. 'Better get some more before ours start.'

Robert walked to the window and looked down. 'You don't know about Hansford, then?'

166

Tim listened in silence.

'Maybe he was trying out a different escape route. Maybe he was really escaping. Maybe he was just drunk.' Robert spoke flatly and unemotionally. 'They thought he was dead at first. No one knows how long he was there for, nor how bad it is. He could be dead now.'

Tim switched off his record. 'He couldn't really have been escaping. I mean, it wasn't really like that. There was no need.'

'Maybe he was practising.'

'At that time of night?'

'He was a funny bloke.'

'Not that funny.'

'He used to get up early to work.'

'That's pretty funny, I admit.'

Tim edged the curtains back from his own windows. 'Broken bones?'

'Don't know. I heard this knocking but I sort of dreamed it was Chetwynd come back for more. Except with Hansford's voice.'

'More what?'

'More whisky. I told you.'

Tim nodded abstractedly. 'And how was Chetwynd?'

'All wired up and calm as the dead. Talked about God. He'd seen us go into chapel. Should have sent him to you.'

'God should have been at Nuremberg.'

'Your second step to conversion.'

Tim switched on the kettle and got out his coffee jug. 'So what else is new?'

'Nothing. Gina and I did it on High Table.'

Tim stopped what he was doing for a moment, then continued as if determined not to be impressed. 'What for?'

'Felt like it. No, that's not true. I suppose I was trying to be different or interesting or something.' He thought of his torn-up application form. 'Making some sort of point.'

167

'What did she make of it?'

'Not much.' Robert went to the door. 'Well, we got away from talking about Hansford easily enough.'

'Life must go on.'

'Must it?'

'Have some coffee then.'

'Not now.'

'Drop in later. Start the day again for me. This one's only twenty minutes old and I don't like it.'

Orpwood was shaken by what had happened. He talked to everyone he met, repeating himself, his eyes earnest and wide. 'I didn't like the bloke or what he stood for but I wouldn't have wished that on him. If he really thought we were out, you know, to kill him, that just shows the extent of his paranoia. I said that to the fuzz and they got annoyed because they couldn't spell it. An hour they were on at me and I've got to see them again. Trouble is, they think I'm the only one with a motive. But as I said to them, what would a big bloke like him be running away from a little bloke like me for?'

He and Robert were standing near the lodge and the college clock struck the quarter. 'Bloody fuzz made me late. Then I had to see the President. I was supposed to go to a revision class up in St Anne's. It's not worth going all that way now.'

Like many in Oxford, he regarded anywhere more than three hundred yards north or south of the High as impossibly far out.

'Borrow my bike if you like.'

'I didn't know you had one.'

'It's in the rack, third from the end.'

Orpwood hurried away. 'Cheers, Robert. Is it locked?'

'No.' He watched Orpwood take it from the place where Hansford had left it.

There were official comings and goings and for a while people were more excited and talkative than usual but the incident made no significant difference to college life. There was some talk of a vendetta, a political killing, a reign of terror, but no one took it seriously and the evening paper reported the event as a student prank gone wrong. Opinion was that Hansford had been practising his escape route while drunk. There was talk of a coma.

'Could it be he caught sight of Chetwynd in subfusc at four in the morning?' asked Tim. 'Or heard him on the stairs?'

'Maybe it was his way of getting out of Schools,' said Robert. No one had suggested suicide. 'Last year a bloke in Corpus stabbed himself with a bread knife.'

'Very appropriate.'

'Do you think you're callous?'

Tim thought. 'Not so callous as to feign feeling.'

Hansford recovered consciousness but it was said that it would be some days before it was known whether he would move his legs again. Interest lessened. Personal concerns reasserted their dominance over the public except for those, such as Orpwood, who made the public personal.

Chapter Ten

The Changeling was not good enough — never that — but by first night it was as good as Robert could make it. The dress rehearsal had been very bad, a favourable sign because dress rehearsals that went well were supposedly followed by anti-climactic first nights.

The play had already attracted a good deal of attention. In a city where theatre audiences were larger and more informed than most and casts more intelligent and enthusiastic — if sometimes lacking in technique — the unusual and the ambitious were given generous hearing. Michael Mann was to review the production for *Isis*.

Robert was as eager and frightened as the rest of the cast but the need to appear confident gave him no chance to indulge his feelings. As director he had worked to make himself redundant by first night, but now as a leading player he had to shoulder another burden. The strain showed. He not only looked tired but for days his responses were slower. He seemed distracted, remote, lacking energy; almost uninvolved.

He began to pick up when the cast gathered backstage. The expectancy, the making-up, the costumes, the confusions and the panics all contributed to the excitement and gave the play an existence beyond its constituent parts: ephemeral but for a time more real than anything.

Robert sometimes said he thought drama was important because it expressed truths, that its fascination was its power to illumine the most real by adopting the conventions of the unreal. The excitement, he said, was the froth, not the real thing. But when he went front of house that night to see the audience coming in, then backstage, then on stage to check that the flats were secure, his movements and speech quickened and his energy and aggression returned.

While checking the flats he found one that still wobbled at a touch but since no one was supposed to touch it he decided it would have to do. As he turned he collided in the semi-darkness with a fast-moving silent body. They grabbed each other by the arms. The grip on his bare forearm was warm and urgent and it was then that he realized it was Gina. She wore a long, loose dress that swept the floor and her hair was tied at the back so that it could be let down later. The make-up made her features sharp.

'It'll be all right, it'll be all right,' he said several times. It felt inadequate but he could think of nothing else. She said nothing. Her eyes were serious and unquestioning. They held each other for some seconds before she passed on without speaking. He remained where he was, physically weak, feeling he had given more of himself to her then than at any other time.

And it was all right, so far as the audience was concerned. They wanted it to succeed and, apart from one or two lapses, faulty emphases and bungled lines, it did. The mistakes were not obvious to anyone unfamiliar with the play, and the madhouse scenes were played with a zest and pace that hid their defects. Gina was irresistible. For those who had once seen her act it was impossible ever to see her off-stage without looking for that same powerful suggestion, the same flashes of passion, anger and vulnerability. It was impossible, too, to say to what extent these qualities inhered in her everyday life; she seemed all potential but in herself was hard to know.

It was clear, too, that Robert was right to have got rid of Malcolm. Both the play and Gina demanded an other significant presence, and though Robert had neither the range nor the versatility of a good actor he had a certain strength and solidity. He gave to the part a brooding menace, a sometimes careless but never unreflecting destructiveness. It was a disconcerting performance.

Though unnoticed by the audience, there was one moment in the central scene with Gina when his mind went blank and he was lost. It was when she was kneeling, clutching his wrist, imploring him to take her wealth in her stead. Her hair by then was loose, she was gripping his wrist with one hand and with the other pulled at her necklace as if offering herself to be hanged. He was making a short reply to her plea and had said the line, 'Can you weep fate from its determin'd purpose?' when one of the lights caught his eye at an unaccustomed angle, momentarily dazzling him. He hesitated and the next line was gone. He stood with his mouth open.

The faces in the front rows of the audience showed up white and distinct. Gina's grip on his wrist was warm and hard, like her grip on his arm before the play started. He experienced everything with hopeless, hypnotic clarity — his own breathing, his sweat, the stage lights shining through her hair — but his mind encompassed only the thought of his failure, a monstrous, paralysing growth.

Her grip hardened and she dragged herself closer. He had no idea how long the pause lasted. He bent and took hold of her wrist with his other hand as if to break her grip. Her face was clear and passionate but her eyes as they sought his were understanding. Very slightly, she moved her lips to form the words, 'So soon.' The spell broke. 'So soon may you weep me,' he said with merciless deliberation and flung her to the floor. There was no time to appreciate his relief and he finished the act without afterwards recalling ending it.

And so it was done, a truth made manifest. Not even the knowledge that it was transient, that the first night would become second, the second third and so on, could detract. The applause at the end was prolonged and sincere.

Afterwards everyone talked, everyone laughed,

everyone was friends. No matter how tired they were it would take hours to unwind. Robert walked among them, grinning broadly. He put his hands on their shoulders, clasped their waists, ruffled their hair while they kissed each other in supposed emulation of their professional colleagues.

He did not touch Gina but bowed and said with exaggerated formality, 'May I walk you home?'

She was dabbing at her make-up. 'All right.'

His composure left him abruptly. 'I wasn't suggesting anything else.'

She smiled. 'I've got an essay to finish, that's all. I shall want some sleep or it'll be me that's finished by tomorrow night.'

They walked towards Jericho in a light warm rain. The air was fresh, the grass and plants could be smelt and the pavements shone under the streetlamps. He was still excited and cheerful.

'You were very, very good. You held it together. What I always hoped you would do.'

'It felt slow in the second act.'

'The pace dropped, I don't know why. We all seem to affect each other. It picked up, though. But you saved me when I dried. I was lost then, gone completely. If you hadn't done that I'd have still been there.'

She looked at the pavement. 'Why did you chose me?'

'Because you auditioned well.'

'Badly, as I remember.'

'Your face fitted.'

'I don't think it was even that.'

'What do you mean?'

She walked on without answering.

'What do you mean?' he asked again.

'It doesn't really work between you and me,' she said. 'It does up to a point because you're aggressive and dramatic but there's no development between us. There's no room for it. You set the terms at the start and that's

173

how it stays. It's exciting but it's not sensitive and flexible. It can't grow.'

He made himself flippant. 'You're talking about on stage?'

'That's what I was talking about,' she said very carefully.

He tried hard to get her to be explicit, analysing his part, pulling it to pieces. She would not be drawn, though, and would say only, 'Forget about yourself. It's in the way.'

Robert fell silent for a while. Eventually he said, 'You make me feel inferior to the character I'm playing, as if I'm letting someone down.' His manner was again flippant but she said nothing and they walked the rest of the way in silence.

At her door he went to follow her in. She stopped. 'I've got an essay, I told you.'

He felt a sudden, immense weariness. 'You don't want to?'

'I didn't say that.'

'But you don't?'

She looked at him quizzically. He regretted the High Table incident, despite her compliance. He had an urgent and almost overwhelming desire, not so much for her as for himself to be wanted.

'I want you,' he said thickly.

'You don't know what you want.'

'I do.' He repeated it several times, more desperately as the untruth became more obvious.

She stopped him by taking his hand and smiling. 'You silly. But not for long, mind. I'm serious about the essay.'

Robert found Tim in his room as usual that night but it was in a state of rare disorder. Books and record covers were on the floor, the curtains were closed, the windows open, the teapot was on the chair, its lid upside down on the table. The music centre blasted Beethoven's Sixth.

Tim sprawled in his armchair, a whisky bottle in one hand and a breadknife in the other. He held the knife by

174

the blade and used it as a conductor's baton. He did not at first appear to notice Robert's arrival but after some seconds held up the whisky and pointed with the knife at the teapot. The pot was still warm. Robert poured tea into one of the dirty cups.

Tim conducted until the record switched itself off. In the silence that followed they could hear the rain on the windowsill. Tim let the knife slip through his fingers until he was holding the point between thumb and forefinger then flicked it up into the air. It rose almost to the ceiling, turned lazily and fell towards his thigh. He watched, unmoving. It half-turned once more, struck his thigh with the handle and bounced against the gas fire.

The tea was cold.

'How'd it go?' Tim asked drowsily.

'Not bad for first night. It'll get better.'

'When should I see it?'

'Give it two more nights.'

Tim drank and proffered the bottle. Robert shook his head. 'Tea's fine.'

There was a long pause. 'Seen Suzanne?'

'Not since we three went to Wytham. Something about that day put her off, more off than she was.'

Robert again remembered her with David Long outside the Union. 'It was our not getting out of the way of that car. Too self-destructive. Women don't like that.'

'Thought it might have turned her on. You know, sympathy, save a soul and all that. Wish I were an anguished monk. She'd prefer that.'

'You still could be.'

'Wouldn't believe me. Wouldn't believe anything I said. Probably wouldn't believe anything I did, either. Always say there's some other reason. Don't blame her.' He smiled. 'But we send letters and notes daily. She's coming to the Merton Ball with me.'

'Well, that's something.'

'If she doesn't change her mind. Have some whisky.'

'Tea's fine.'

Tim leaned forward holding the bottle unsteadily. 'Please.'

Robert emptied his tea back into the pot and held out his cup.

'To Hansford.' said Tim. 'I hear he's up and in a wheelchair.'

'And to the cat.'

'I'd forgotten the cat.'

It was raining harder. 'I want to walk. Come with me? Make sure I get back, you know.'

'Where?'

'Tell you when we get there.' He took a silver hip-flask from his cupboard and filled it with whisky. 'Bottle's a bit ostentatious, don't you think?'

'Are you rich or very rich?'

'Family money plus two rich stepfathers, plus shares in the distillery.'

They walked for about twenty minutes in the steady rain. Tim took regular swigs from the flask. Robert had one every other time. When Tim stopped to pee in the shadow of Magdalen Wall Robert leaned against the lamp-post, pressing the back of his head against it and looking up at the rain.

Tim emerged haltingly from the shadow. 'Feels like I peed in my pants.'

'Maybe you did.'

'Not sure it was even me that peed.' Never trust what I feel.'

They climbed back in the way Robert had come with Hansford, this time avoiding the dustbins. The Jaguar was still in the don's car park and yet more notices had been stuck on it. There was only one small part of the windscreen uncovered.

'I suppose I could move it now.'

'If it'll start.'

'Gate's locked.'

Robert moved off but Tim remained by the car, his hand on the roof. He looked very pale. 'I'm going to throw up.'

'Don't do it there, do it on the grass.' said Robert quickly.

Tim shook his head. 'Can't move.'

Robert took him round the waist, keeping himself behind, then moved him carefully across the grass to the cherry tree. He propped him up against it and stepped back. 'Go on, then.'

Tim bent but did not retch. His pallor showed even in the dark. He shook his head again. 'Can't. Want to but can't.'

'Put your finger in your throat.'

Tim tried a couple of times, ineffectually. 'Squeamish.'

Standing to one side, Robert took him by the hair and with his other hand poked his fingers into his mouth. Tim's abdomen contracted immediately. Robert took out his hand and Tim vomited. Robert held him by the collar until he was finished. Tim wiped his chin with grass. 'Friendship. Thanks.'

Robert wiped his own fingers with grass though there was no need. 'Do the same for me one day.'

'I hope not.'

Chapter Eleven

The talks in Geneva continued for the rest of the week. There were no press releases beyond details of at what times meetings had taken place and how long they had lasted. Radio and television journalists had to make do with interviewing each other while the newspapers ran such headlines as, 'World Leaders Talk on Brink of Doom', 'War or Peace — Latest', 'World: Is End Near?' and 'Crisis: EEC to Meet Soon'. The hot weather continued.

Once the play had started Robert had more time to himself. There were no more rehearsals and each day revolved around the evening performance. He seemed to find even the ordinary routines of life an effort. He avoided conversation, didn't bother to collect his *Times* and moved the Jaguar only as far as the space behind the kitchens, where it began to collect more notices. The President sent a letter threatening action. Meanwhile, he spent much of each day dozing on the grass of the Fellows Garden, his books beside him. In the late afternoons he went for runs that were longer and harder than ever.

Tim, on the other hand, seemed to be forever preparing for work — he journeyed to and from the library, carried books to and from his room, cleaned his bicycle, started the BMW, polished it, made lists, visited the Bodleian — but was not once seen to do any. Early on the last night of the play he appeared in Robert's room wearing a double-breasted dinner jacket.

'Have a nice play.'

'Have a nice ball.'

'I'm trying hard not to let it distract me from our first papers the day after tomorrow. Like hell I am. How's Gina?'

'Acting well.'

'And the real Gina? Or is that too subtle a distinction?'

'Tell you next week.'

'At the moment I don't feel there's going to be a next week.'

Tim made a minute adjustment to his bow-tie, then produced his hip-flask.

'You're drinking more than you did,' said Robert.

Tim poured carefully into the outer cup. 'If you're up to it tomorrow afternoon, why don't we meet Chetwynd outside Schools? It's his last paper. I want to see how he coped. If he can do it we can. Possibly.'

'Give him his gun and his bullet.'

'I'm getting fond of that gun. Take it out and feel it now and then. Good luck tonight.' He handed Robert the cup and swigged from the flask.

Suzanne's dress was of long black silk, high-necked and sleeved and tightly waisted. The cuffs and neck were edged with white lace and a red rose was pinned above her breast. Her hair just failed to conceal two very small gold earings, each with a tiny pale blue stone. She looked thinner in the face and nervous.

She held up part of the dress for Tim to see. 'I hope this is all right. It's very old.'

'It's very beautiful.'

'It belonged to my grandmother and I altered it.'

'It really is beautiful.'

'Do you mean that?'

'Yes.'

'Would you like some sherry or something, or had we better go?'

'We'd better go.'

'I bought the rose because I knew it wasn't safe to rely on you.'

179

She took a black woollen shawl and they set off arm in arm for Merton. He felt happier than for months. It was remarkably simple — the touch of a woman's arm. He even encouraged her to talk of Schools, which she had just finished.

Eventually she said, 'Don't make me talk about Schools. I shall go on about them all evening and spoil everything. Tell me what you've been doing. I'm so happy I could fly.'

The ball was smaller than most, and better. A band and disco alternated in the Great Hall, and food was so arranged that there were no queues. The sitting out rooms, recently vacated by people who had gone down early, had uneven floors and oak beams and were reached by narrow winding wooden staircases. They had never danced together and agreed to do so straight away so as not to go on feeling awkward about it.

It was disco music, and convention demanded a form of on-the-spot jogging independently of each other. Tim called it monkey-scratching and imitated the solemn or vacuous expressions of the other dancers. She didn't realize he was imitating them and when he smiled to show that he was she smiled back awkwardly.

'I'm happy, that's all, he said.'

A slower number meant they could do a sideways shuffle that they both pretended was a waltz. Her body was warm through the silk dress. 'Do you remember my telling you not to come and see me again?' she asked.

'Vividly.'

She laughed. 'I really meant it, you know. I really did.'

'I really believed you.'

'How's Robert?'

'He's okay.'

'I don't how you can be so unworried about Schools.'

'I'd like a drink.'

There were people they knew but no one to whom they felt obliged to talk. The night was one of the shortest of the year and they spent much of it dancing. In the dawn they wandered along the top of the garden wall that overlooked Christ Church meadows. There was a heavy dew and a white mist hung low over the Thames.

She leaned against the wall, her back to the meadow. 'I wonder if our fate has been decided.'

'What do you mean?'

'The summit conference. It was going on all night. Don't you pay any attention to the news?'

'Oh, yes. Well, it'll be all right.'

She smiled. 'It will, will it?'

'The world will go on. Tomorrow and tomorrow and tomorrow.'

'We might not go on with it.'

'We won't anyway.'

'Speak for yourself.' She kissed him lightly and they walked farther along the wall. The willows by the river loomed out of the mist. She clasped his arm and pressed her head against his shoulder.

'Shall we go home?'

Logic Lane, the High and Magdalen bridge were peopled by dawdling couples, the long dresses of the girls and the black jackets of the men sharp and clear in the early light. The hazy sun picked out yellows and browns in the grey stonework. At the bridge itself a noisy party had stolen one of the punts and was trying to take it downstream without a pole, using champagne bottles to steer. Each time it wobbled the men roared and the girls squealed, holding up their dresses.

The curtains were drawn in her room and it was nearly dark. She turned towards him with a deliberate smile that made her look, for a moment, quite unlike herself.

He woke a few hours later, his arm and shoulder painfully stiff. With great care he removed them from beneath her head. She had slept deeply and he badly in the narrow bed. It had been good, they had been closer than ever, closer than he had thought they could be, but too late. In his heart he was indifferent, cold and incapable. It was not that he no longer wanted her but that he no longer wanted.

He got up quietly and peered through the curtains at yet another cloudless day. He sorted out their scattered clothes into separate heaps, laying her dress carefully on the window seat, then moved silently round the room gathering cups, tea, kettle.

Asleep, she looked vulnerable and girlish. When he had made tea he woke her by touching her shoulder. 'Powdered milk. Sorry.'

She propped herself up on her elbow, blinking and rubbing her bleary eyes. Her features now were pasty and slack. 'What time is it?'

'Eleven.'

She groaned. 'I'm supposed to be at David Long's lunch party in an hour.'

He had to be careful not to show his relief. He put on his black trousers and white shirt and went out to get milk, realizing from the shop girl's smile that he had forgotten to comb his hair. On the way back he decided to get a new BMW when Schools were over. It was refreshing to think of such things. When he returned they had cereal and more tea.

She showered and put on a skirt and blouse. He felt unreachably distant, sorry for her, guilty, anxious to be away, and so was more than normally affectionate. She put on more make-up than usual.

The lunch party was at Exeter. He walked with her, his dinner-jacket over his shoulder and his bow-tie hanging from his pocket.

'We must look very obvious,' she said.

'May as well flaunt it.'

'You enjoy that, don't you?'

They kissed goodbye outside the college. 'We shouldn't see any more of each other until your Schools are over. You must give yourself a chance.'

'It doesn't make any difference.'

'Tim, don't be so stupid. You've got to try.'

182

He said he would come for tea after the first day. She said no. He argued with growing force as fear of his own selfishness gripped him. Minutes before he had been glad at the thought of getting away but now he insisted on seeing her as soon as possible. She relented while he was in mid-sentence, smiling suddenly and laying her hand affectionately on his arm. 'Tea would be lovely.'

It was the only arrangement he made for anything after Schools.

Chapter Twelve

The last night of 'The Changeling was not as good as the one before. The cast was anticipating the sensation of climax and did not concentrate fully. But the audience was the most responsive they had had, and the applause prolonged. Everyone was exhausted and exhilarated, and celebrations began before the set was struck. The cast party was to be held on stage.

Michael Mann's *Isis* review had been more generous than Robert had hoped. There was some just criticism of the madhouse scenes, but Michael had concluded that the essence of the play, the central relationship, had come over powerfully and well. Malcolm had reviewed the play for *Cherwell*, without malice but without mentioning Robert.

'And I meant it,' Michael Mann said on stage afterwards, grinning and putting his hand on Robert's shoulder.

'That's good.' Robert caught Gina's eye. 'Glad you said it worked, but it's nice to know you meant it, too.'

'Did you really think so?' asked Gina.

Michael's smile made his eyes disappear. 'Really.'

He turned again to Robert. 'Good news about Anne.'

'What?'

'The baby. She's had it. I ran into Dr Barry then I went up to see her. She's looking well.'

One of the flats came down with a crash and there was a cheer. Wine appeared and there was another outbreak of kissing and embracing. Robert went through the motions of participation until he came back to Gina. She was still wearing her gown and was starting to take off her make-up.

'Well, we got away with it, ' he said. 'Though that's not as it should be.'

'It's the way most things are, isn't it?'

He stood as if waiting for something. 'It's hard to believe I'm starting Schools the day after tomorrow. I won't really believe it until I'm sitting there.'

She shook her hair. 'Why didn't you go and see Anne?'

'I can't, with this party.'

'You could if you slip away now.'

'And come back later, yes.' It was what he had wanted but he still did not move. 'And tomorrow, let's do something. You and me. Go out of Oxford. I'll come round.'

With both hands she gathered her hair behind her neck and spread it again.

He ran back to college for the Jaguar. It was likely he had missed visiting hours, but he would try anyway. The engine turned reluctantly. He swore at the battery and gave it a rest while he peeled off the Bursar's 'No Parking' stickers. He thought of Tim's BMW but Tim was at the ball. He thought of a taxi but there was the cash problem and by now he was locked into an obstinate struggle with the Jaguar, cursing the absence of starting handles on cars of post–1950s design.

The engine fired unexpectedly on the last turn of the tired battery and he set off for the hospital amid clouds of blue smoke and near-constant misfiring. No florists were open. He braked hard when he saw roses in a garden in Summertown. His first thought was to steal them but he resolved to be honourable and to try to buy them from the owner. There was no one in. He considered theft but someone next door was looking through the front window. He ended up with a faded box of Black Magic from a nearby pub.

At the hospital he gave her name to the girl at reception who said she had no record. She made a telephone call, then another, breaking off to say, 'You're Dr Barry, are you?'

'Sorry?'

'You're her husband?'

'No. I've just come to see her. To see if she's all right. I'm a friend.'

'He wants to know how she's getting on,' the girl said into the receiver. 'They're just checking. Sorry to keep you. We're not supposed to let any more visitors in, really.'

He leaned against the desk and picked at a splinter of wood. Hospitals horrified him. He dreaded being told it had been a difficult birth.

The girl put down the telephone. 'Yes, she's in Ward Three. Straight through and second left and up the stairs.'

'What is it?'

'What is what?'

'The baby.'

'I don't know. You'll have to ask.'

Two men walked briskly out through the swing doors, one laughing loudly.

'She's okay, is she?'

'Oh yes, I think so. All quite normal, I expect. You weren't present, then?'

'Present?'

'At the birth. You know, a lot of people are. It's the fashion nowadays.'

He found the ward at the second attempt and stood clutching his Black Magic in the entrance, unable to see her because there were so many women. It was her smile that pulled his eyes back to her. She was a third of the way down, propped up in bed in a red nightgown, her brown hair unpinned and spread over her shoulders. She continued smiling at him. As he approached she closed the book she was reading and put it on the bedside table.

'Are you all right?'

'I've never felt better.'

'And the baby?'

'Eight pounds eight ounces of bouncing boy.'

'Really?'

He stood, grinning and nodding.

She pointed to the chair. 'Why don't you sit down?'

Flowers were on the table, on the locker, on the floor: mostly roses. It looked as if she'd been placed among them for filming. Many people must have been already. He pushed the Black Magic along the bed, feeling inadequate and grubby. 'I only heard just now and came straight up. All the florists were closed. This was all I could find.'

'Thank you. I've been told I must eat a lot.' She put the box prominently on the table.

'I'll bring you some flowers tomorrow.'

'Don't worry — you bought some the other day, remember? When I didn't want to talk to you.'

'Yes, well, sorry about that.'

'Don't be. You're very sweet.'

He felt clumsy and superfluous. 'How was it?'

'Much better than I'd thought. Very quick and easy. Almost too quick. I nearly didn't make it to the hospital. David drove me. I think he was more frightened than I was.' She laughed.

'Lucky he was there.'

'Yes, it was.'

He clasped his hands and looked at the floor. 'What are you going to call him?'

'I'm not sure yet, I keep thinking. I think James or Michael. Perhaps Michael James.'

A nurse called for visitors to leave. 'I'll come again tomorrow. What's a good time?'

'You have to go now. You can see him on the way out. Ask the nurse to show you.'

He stood. 'He's not in here, then?'

'No, not yet. You'd know it if he was.'

'I'll bring a little present or something when I come tomorrow.'

'No, don't. Please don't come tomorrow.'

187

'Why not?' He knew he sounded abrupt.

Her expression was direct and thoughtful. 'I'd rather you didn't come at all, Robert.' she said quietly. 'I'm very fond of you but it would be better if you stayed away. Please understand.' The nurse was hurrying people out. The woman in the next bed stared with uninhibited curiosity. 'It's David, ' she continued, seeing him unmoving.

'But he's not jealous. He doesn't mind, does he?' He thought of the Bursar's secretary. It would be so easy. 'He doesn't mind, does he?' he repeated challengingly.

She shook her head. 'It's not just him, it's me as well. I'm very fond of you, Robert, I really am, but I'm going to be very taken up. There's not much of me to go round. Perhaps after a couple of months.' She smiled brightly. 'Come and see me then.'

'Whose is it?' he asked slowly.

Her smile did not fade entirely. 'Robert, you don't really mind, you don't really care, do you? Not in your heart of hearts. Do you? It doesn't make a difference to you. Nobody does.'

He stared and said nothing.

'He's mine,' she continued. 'That's what matters.'

He turned and walked back down the ward.

'You want to see the baby?' the nurse asked pleasantly. She led him to a side ward where there were babies in cots and pointed at one which had 'Baby Barry' written on a disk tied to his ankle. 'He's quiet now, but he's going to be a handful, that one. Full of life.' She left him. The baby was surprisingly small. He had a few wisps of dark hair, his head was turned to the side and his eyes were closed. Robert bent and with great care touched the baby's temple with his finger. It was soft and warm. The baby did not open his eyes.

'Come along now, please,' called another nurse. 'Visitors out, please.'

He left the hospital and walked fast, at first towards and then on past the Jaguar. An American he knew was cycling in the other direction and shouted across the street but Robert kept walking.

It was not that he neither knew nor cared where he went though that was an impression he might have been content to give. Woodstock was eight or ten miles away and it took determination rather than carelessness to walk there. Nor did he forget about the Jaguar; rather, he decided to abandon it.

The northward sprawl of Oxford and the incessant headlights made for a walk that was neither enjoyable nor peaceful but that did not matter. By the time he reached Woodstock he was gratifyingly weary. He trudged through the streets of Cotswold stone buildings, then through the gates and into the grounds of Blenheim Palace. He left the drive and headed across the grass into the dark. The confidence and scale of the palace and grounds had long appealed to him, and he and Tim had once unsuccessfully applied for a flat there. They would have enjoyed the address.

The night was warm, the grass damp. His shoes and socks were soon soaked. There was a crescent moon and once his eyes had adjusted he could see surprisingly far. From down by the lake came the muted calls of ducks and moorhens and occasionally the sounds of other birds he could not identify.

He trod a wide circle round the back of the palace in search of some where to sleep. Wet now as well as weary, he felt as he imagined vagabonds felt as he crept cautiously into a wooden shed. Having established there were no large beasts he lay down on a pile of paper sacks that smelt of animal food. He dozed fitfully, disturbed by the rustlings of small creatures, the discomfort of his bed and, towards dawn, the cold.

By daylight the vagabond sensation had not lost all its appeal but he needed no further taste of it. He walked down through the wet grass to a secluded part of the lake. The morning was still and unbroken. He stripped and stepped determinedly into the cold water, having to

189

wade some way out, treading mud and leaves, until it was deep enough to swim. It was very cold and not at all enjoyable but when he dressed afterwards he felt a temporary warmth and vigour. A herd of Sussex bullocks, with glistening red-brown coats and breath steaming from their wide nostrils, gazed incuriously as he loped through the grass towards the town, shoes and socks in his hands and his trousers rolled up to his knees.

There was no answer to his knock on Gina's window. He thought she might still be in bed and he knocked loudly on the door.

It was opened by a fair-haired man from Hertford, eating toast. 'Gone down,' he answered immediately. Robert stared. 'Gone down, gone home.' The man swallowed. 'She packed late last night and left first thing this morning. Back next term.'

The aptness almost made him smile. Her timing was always perfect. He knew before asking that there would be no message. He would have liked to congratulate her.

'The college will have her address, ' the man added.

Robert walked slowly away, feeling now that the last strand had snapped. It was a matter neither for regret nor relief. Already it felt inevitable, part of a process. The pity was that he would have liked to talk to her about it.

At lunchtime in the porter's lodge he found another letter from his father and a note from the Bursar. He left the latter in his pigeon-hole and took his copy of *The Times*. The headlines announced that the two super powers were on the point of agreement. There was world-wide relief and bishops gave thanks. He reflected that it might have been better for Hansford to have joined the army after all.

He ran into Tim in the quad. Their exchange of explanations was brief and spare.

'I'm starving,' Robert said.

'Pubs are open'

'Bath first.'

'Join me down there. It's Chetwynd's last paper, remember? We could meet him. I've got some champagne.'

Robert threw Tim *The Times* as they parted. 'Celebrate that while you're waiting. Good news about the world.'

'What?'

'It's been saved.' Tim looked blank. 'The summit. No nuclear war.'

'Great.'

On his door was a note from the Chaplain asking about his application for theological college. The application form was still in pieces on his desk. He started idly putting them together but then, with one movement of his arms, swept them into the waste paper bin.

Chapter Thirteen

There was already a crowd of several hundred by the side entrance to the Schools building. Those who had finished their last papers were met by friends, often with champagne. The crowd blocked the lane because the Bulldogs allowed no one through the wrought-iron gates.

On this day the crowd was particularly boisterous, perhaps because of the good news from Geneva. Three harassed policemen tried to keep people from spilling on to the High. Bulldogs, to cheers and jeers, strove energetically to keep others from climbing the gates and railings.

At 5.30 the doors opened and the gowned figures poured out. There was a cheer, followed by champagne corks and a reciprocal launching of mortar-boards into the air. Chetwynd had not known he was to be met and was at first confused, then for once, embarrassed.

He recovered quickly. 'How kind. This is the nearest I shall get to celebrating my own funeral.' The champagne popped and frothed. He poured it into his mortar-board. 'Will you take communion with me?' He held it delicately by two corners, drank and passed it round. They were jostled by the crowd and finished with wet faces and shirts. When the cap was empty he put it back on his head.

They pushed their way onto the High. The three policemen had good-naturedly given up any serious attempt to control the crowd. The rush hour traffic was halted in both directions as undergraduates wandered through it and over it in peaceful anarchy.

Chetwynd talked. 'I was there for every damn paper.

God alone knows how. My last answer was a verse imitation of Tennyson. I can't even remember the questions. Give me the bottle. We'll need another.'

'At least you did it,' said Tim. 'If you can, maybe we can.'

'Masturbation is the answer. A private and irrefutable assertion of self against the world. It takes the edge off anxiety and everything else, especially feelings of the heart. But not too often otherwise it's monotonous and depressing. It also helps cope with sitting next to women in subfusc. Your papers start tomorrow afternoon, don't they? Hours away. We must drink deeply.'

'I was going to work,' said Tim.

'Robert?'

'So was I.'

Chetwynd grinned. 'You are admirable and hopeless, both of you.'

They walked through Magdalen and along Addison's Walk, then followed the footpath up to the Cherwell Boathouse where Chetwynd bought wine.

They took a punt upstream to the Victoria Arms, sat in the garden and drank beer. On the way back Chetwynd recited *The Ancient Mariner* in a fluctuating French accent.

They had more wine at the boathouse, called for a taxi which didn't come, called another and went to the Elizabeth for dinner. Tim paid by credit card. He seemed relaxed and remote, careless of everything.

Robert was equally careless but showed it by arguing energetically and arbitrarily with Chetwynd about subjects that did not matter to him — impressionism, capital punishment, Buster Keaton, pacifism — until Chetwynd became maudlin and talked with uncharacteristic incoherence about the death of his father, the vicar.

'Learn to love necessity, ' he concluded abruptly, as if sober.

'Why?' asked Robert.

'It's all there is.'

They stayed late and left only after Chetwynd was rude

to one of the waiters whom he said was homosexual and trying not to be. They walked back arm in arm.

'We'll lay you out in your crypt,' said Tim.

'Come down by all means but don't lay me to rest. Help me to pack. Tonight I'm driving to Shropshire.'

'You're drunk, you can't.'

'I am and I can. I must leave Oxford tonight. I want to leave it as I am now. I shall never come back. This is how I want to remember.'

He parked his Ford van illegally in the quad and they helped him pack. There was not much.

The Chaplain found them. 'Dark deeds in the night, gentlemen? I thought you were sacking the chapel.' He stood a few yards off, smiling enigmatically but speaking with a heartiness that seemed foreign to him. He asked the sorts of questions about Schools that everyone asked, then shook hands with Chetwynd. 'Do keep in touch.' He turned to Tim and Robert. 'Good luck tomorrow. Come and have a night cap when you've finished here if it's not too late.'

'He looked awkward,' said Tim when he had gone. 'As if he didn't really want to invite us.'

'Because of what we're doing,' said Robert.

'No. Because he stays and we go, ' said Chetwynd 'Different worlds now. We shared his, now we're leaving it. Intimations of mortality.'

'Talking of which,' Robert struggled with his jeans pocket. 'Your bullet, look, and your gun. We'd better get it.'

Chetwynd stared at the little bullet. 'Keep them both. Throw them into the Cherwell.'

'You think you won't need them now Schools are over?'

Chetwynd still stared at it. 'No more gestures. If I want to do it I shall jump over a cliff. Otherwise I shall rot in my vicarage and go mad more quietly than here. This place has always been bad for me. It's not real but it hurts.' He held up his hand. 'Goodbye. You have helped make it endurable. No formalities. Better to part when drunk. The college has my address, if ever you are inclined. Live well and be selfish.'

The starter motor grated but worked at the fifth or sixth attempt. They watched him edge uncertainly round the quad and out through the lodge, knocking over the blackboard.

The Chaplain seemed a little surprised when they called, as if he had not really expected them. 'Come in, come in,' he said, waving his hand, again with unusual heartiness.

They had brandies. Tim sat in the same chair as when he had come to talk about the President's sermon, slowly turning the brandy round in its large glass. Robert stood looking at the books, his back towards the others.

The Chaplain raised his glass. 'We should toast our mutual friend, Chetwynd, an — ' he hesitated over the word and smiled — 'original man.'

Robert drank without looking round. The Chaplain glanced at his back. 'Accidie, Robert?'

Robert raised his glass in acknowledgement.

'Translate for Tim,' the Chaplain continued.

'Sloth.'

'More precisely, that state of negligence and indifference in which a man may neither work nor pray. One of the Seven Deadly Sins. "Sloth" does not quite do it justice. I was reminded the other day by your application, Robert, or lack of it.'

Robert turned and smiled without humour. 'I plead guilty to accidie.'

'Makes very little difference how you plead.' The Chaplain's blue eyes twinkled at Tim. 'It's that noonday devil again, you know. Very catching.'

'I was trying to think of the other six,' said Tim.

The Chaplain laughed, 'One is all you need. Like love in the Beatles song.'

When they left he walked out with them into the quad. The night was relatively cool. Broken clouds scurried over the chapel roof. 'Well, your last night, gentlemen — before Schools, I mean. Good luck.'

Tim put his hands behind his head and stretched. The quad was deserted. Only three lights were on in the Old Building.

Robert turned to the Chaplain. 'Which of the Seven is yours?'

'Pride.'

'What do you do about it?'

'Pray,' The Chaplain spoke quickly, his slim face visible only in outline. 'It's all you can ever do. Even if you can't mean it you must do it. It's all there is.'

'That's what Chetwynd said about necessity.'

'Prayer reveals the necessary. One small step towards God.' He held up his hands as if in blessing. 'Good luck with your papers. May Norrington be with you.' He laughed briefly and turned away.

The sun was subversive of all endeavour and it was hard for anyone to remain inside. For those with Schools the weather was cruel.

Tim lay in the Fellows Garden for much of that last morning. Various people spoke to him. They found him relaxed and, they thought, needlessly modest about his chances. He had a good mathematical mind and would certainly have no trouble with the logic but he was quoted as saying that the chapter headings now read like epitaphs to what he once had known. At least, he had known what was thought to be right and thought to be wrong about Hume on causality but he had never entered into it and made it his own, had never understood why Hume thought as he did and why he was both right and wrong.

Robert's paper was on Isaiah and Deuteronomy though he sat reading Ecclesiastes. It was hard to see anything Christian in the book but it told men how to live and how little to expect and he liked it for that. He turned then to Job, again using the King James's version. The translation from the Hebrew was narrower than the Greek but seemed more essential. It was the simple strong prose of men who believed and who were unafraid to name things. Yet ultimately it was not their style that drew him but their faith. The style embodied the faith.

Later, in a spasm of thoughtfulness, he went out and bought two red carnations, giving one to Tim.

'Traditionally they should be white, red only on the last day,' said Tim, who knew about such things.

'May as well go down with flags flying.'

They lunched together in Hall, already in dark suits and polished shoes. Robert had broken the elastic on his clip-on white bow tie and had had to borrow a proper one, which Tim had to tie for him. They decided to be late. There was always a nervous crush of people outside the Schools building waiting for the doors to open and they were determined to avoid it. Candidates were allowed to be up to thirty minutes late for each paper.

'Flags flying,' Tim had said when asked why they were dawdling over lunch.

The examination began at 2.30 and they passed through the porters lodge five minutes after that, wearing gowns, carnations in their button holes. In the lodge there was a letter for Robert in a woman's hand. He must have seen but he did not take it out. His car had been towed away from outside the hospital that morning though it was not clear whether or not he knew. They walked in step, hands behind their backs, slowly enough for their gowns to hang straight. On the High they were filmed by Japanese tourists.

'Feels like a real execution,' said Tim.

There was a solitary figure outside the entrance to Schools. When they got closer they saw it was Orpwood. His gown was half off one shoulder, his face was white and he was either sweating or crying. He was turning the pages of a book desperately and hopelessly and leant against the wall for support.

'I revised the wrong bloody paper,' he said, almost sobbing. 'It's political history and I thought it was political

197

theory. I've had it now, I've had it for the rest of my life. I'm just doing what I can before the half hour is up.'

Robert put his arm round him. 'You'll be all right. You know more than you think.'

'Go in. Sit down and relax for a while,' said Tim. 'Best thing you can do.'

'It's alright for you two, you don't care,' he said tearfully, and turned away.

Robert put his arm round him again. 'Come on, you'll make it.' Between them they got him in.

Tim paused in the high doorway of his room and politely inclined his head to the invigilator, who nodded. Nearly everyone glanced up as he walked to the only empty desk, probably envying what must have looked like supreme confidence. He unscrewed the cap from his fountain pen, balanced it very precisely on the corner of the desk, then read the questions. They were searching, fair and well formulated. The paper had a modest, scholarly and serious appearance. He would have been very happy to talk about any of the questions; what bored him in examinations was writing his answers. He sat back and gazed at the ornate ceiling. He had never noticed it before. It was a very fine piece of work.

In another room Robert listened to the scratching of pens, stared at the girl in front, then at other girls, but saw no chance of serious distraction. Through the half-open door that led to the next room he could just see Hansford in a wheelchair, writing laboriously. Someone said he could have had an aegrotat but had insisted on sitting his papers, the first in his family who had.

Afterwards they had to push their way through the crowd. Neither spoke until they were on the High.

'So?' said Tim.

'So what?'

'So nothing.'

They passed parties in college gardens.

'We've blown it this time,' Tim said.

198

'So?'

'So nothing.'

'Orpwood left early. I saw him go.'

'He was still in the crowd outside, with Jan Simpson. She kissed him.'

'Maybe he's got there at last.'

Tim sighed. 'I'd thought about leaving but it seemed impolite, having arrived so late. Like missing the starter, picking at your main course and leaving before the pudding. I kept thinking of Chetwynd too. That didn't help.'

'What are we going to do with his gun and bullet?'

'What he said, I suppose.'

'Now?'

Tim thought of Suzanne, with whom he was supposed to have tea. 'So long as we're not seen.'

They took the revolver from Tim's drawer, the bullet from Robert's jeans. Tim stuffed the revolver in his trousers and pulled his gown across in front.

'I feel like a flasher,' he said.

Chetwynd had specified the Cherwell and so they walked up to the parks. There were people on the bridge Robert usually ran over. They continued upstream towards the garden of Lady Margaret Hall.

Robert squinted at the sun on the water. 'Remember when he played Russian roulette in front of us?'

'I feel I've been playing it for months and lost this afternoon. But I never played it like that. Have you?'

'No.'

'Fancy it?' Tim's tone was light.

After a pause, Robert nodded very slightly. 'If you like.'

They sat on the bank near where the Lady Margaret Hall fence ran down to the water's edge. Beyond the trees people were playing tennis. Behind was the pond, a partial shield from the rest of the park. Two women with small children were throwing bread to the ducks which flapped and splashed and fought. First one swan, then another awkwardly left the island in the middle and glided swiftly towards the food.

At the sound of the shot ducks and swans rose clamorously, and the women reached for their children.